Angelique k... and step back... away by the masculine interest that flared to life in Kasim's gaze.

She wasn't falsely modest. She knew she was beautiful. It was one of the reasons camera lenses so often turned on her. Men looked at her with desire all the time. There was no reason she should react to this man's naked hunger. But she did.

A very animalistic sexual reaction pierced deep in her loins, flooding her with heat. And, yes…it was reciprocal desire. He was looking at her as if he found her appealing, and she certainly found him as attractive as they came. There might even be something chemical here, because her gaze dropped involuntarily to his mouth. Longing rose within her.

His lips quirked.

She knew he was reading her reaction and was amused. It stung. She felt raw and gauche. It was the bane of her existence that she couldn't always stop whatever feelings were overtaking her. But this was so intense it was unprecedented, touching her at all levels. Physical, mental, emotional… He held her entire being enthralled.

"We are finished talking," he said, while his arm bent against her grip. His hand arrived at her waist, hot and sure. His other hand tightened slightly on her arm, drawing her forward a half step, commanding, but not forcing. "If you would like to start something new, however…"

Don't, ...th was cc ... in eager ...

The Sauveterre Siblings

Meet the world's most renowned family…

Angelique, Henri, Ramon and Trella—two sets of
twins born to a wealthy French tycoon and his Spanish
aristocrat wife. Fame, notoriety and an excess of
bodyguards is the price of being part of their illustrious
dynasty. And wherever the Sauveterre twins go,
scandal is sure to follow!

They're protected by the best security money can
buy—no one can break through their barriers… But
what happens when each of these Sauveterre siblings
meets the one person who can breach their heart…?

Meet the heirs to the Sauveterre fortune
in Dani Collins's fabulous new quartet:

Pursued by the Desert Prince
March 2017

His Mistress with Two Secrets
April 2017

Ramon and Isadora's story
Coming soon!

Trella and Prince Xavier's story
Coming soon!

PURSUED BY THE DESERT PRINCE

BY
DANI COLLINS

All ... le
or ... nt with
Ha

Th ... and
inc ... eal
life ... ss
est ... ce is
ent

This book is sold subject to the condition that it shall not, by way of trade or otherwise, be lent, resold, hired out or otherwise circulated without the prior consent of the publisher in any form of binding or cover other than that in which it is published and without a similar condition including this condition being imposed on the subsequent purchaser.

® and TM are trademarks owned and used by the trademark owner and/or its licensee. Trademarks marked with ® are registered with the United Kingdom Patent Office and/or the Office for Harmonisation in the Internal Market and in other countries.

First Published in Great Britain 2017
By Mills & Boon, an imprint of HarperCollins*Publishers*
1 London Bridge Street, London, SE1 9GF

© 2017 Dani Collins

ISBN: 978-0-263-92409-1

Our policy is to use papers that are natural, renewable and recyclable products and made from wood grown in sustainable forests. The logging and manufacturing processes conform to the legal environmental regulations of the country of origin.

Printed and bound in Spain
by CPI, Barcelona

Canadian **Dani Collins** knew in high school that she wanted to write romance for a living. Twenty-five years later, after marrying her high school sweetheart, having two kids with him, working at several generic office jobs and submitting countless manuscripts, she got 'The Call'. Her first Mills & Boon novel won the Reviewers' Choice Award for Best First in Series from *RT Book Reviews*. She now works in her own office, writing romance.

Books by Dani Collins

Mills & Boon Modern Romance

The Secret Beneath the Veil
Bought by Her Italian Boss
Vows of Revenge
Seduced into the Greek's World
The Russian's Acquisition
An Heir to Bind Them
A Debt Paid in Passion
More than a Convenient Marriage?
No Longer Forbidden?

The Wrong Heirs

The Marriage He Must Keep
The Consequence He Must Claim

Seven Sexy Sins

The Sheikh's Sinful Seduction

The 21ˢᵗ Century Gentleman's Club

The Ultimate Seduction

One Night With Consequences

Proof of Their Sin

Visit the Author Profile page
at millsandboon.co.uk for more titles.

Dear Reader,

I've always found the idea of being a twin fascinating. I especially love the stories you sometimes hear of a particular pair having a subliminal connection, even when distance separates them. Or the smaller, simpler things—like a pair inventing their own language or dressing the same without consulting the other.

I brought all this to my new quartet, The Sauveterre Siblings. They're a wealthy family who have been blessed with identical twin boys and then a pair of identical twin girls. The press are mad for them. They followed the children's every move, and only grew worse after the youngest was kidnapped when she was nine. Trella was returned to them, but they all wear the scars.

In this first story Angelique is still trying to find who she might have been if her sister had never been torn from her. Kasim has his own demons created by a lost sibling. Their worlds are very different, but they're drawn inexorably into an affair that is only meant to last one night.

I hope you enjoy watching the Sauveterre twins find that special someone who will help each of them heal from their past.

Dani

To my sisters, who often live far away,
but remain close, close, close in my heart.
Love yous. xoxo

CHAPTER ONE

ANGELIQUE SAUVETERRE PICKED up a call from her exterior guards informing her that Kasim ibn Nour, Crown Prince of Zhamair, had arrived to see her.

She slumped back in her chair with a sigh, really not up to meeting someone new. Not after today.

"Of course. Please show him up to my office," she said. Because she had to.

Hasna had said her brother would drop by while he was in Paris.

Angelique didn't know why the brother of the bride wanted to meet the designer of the bride's wedding gown, but she assumed he wanted to arrange a surprise gift. So she didn't expect this meeting to be long or awful. Her *day* with Princess Hasna and the bridal party hadn't been awful. It had actually been quite pleasant.

It was just a lot of people and noise and Angelique was an introvert. When she told people that, they always said, *But you're not shy!* She had been horribly shy as a child, though, and brutally forced to get over it. Now she could work a room with the best of them, but it fried her down to a crisp.

She yearned for the day when her sister, Trella, would be ready to be the face of Maison des Jumeaux. An ironic thought, since her twin wore the same face.

As she freshened "their" lipstick, Angelique acknowledged that she really longed for Trella to be the one to talk to new clients and meet with brothers of the bride and put on fetes like the one she'd hosted today.

She wanted Trella to be all better.

But she wouldn't press. Trella had made such progress getting over her phobias, especially in the past year. She was determined to attend Hasna and Sadiq's wedding and was showing promise in getting there.

It will happen, Angelique reassured herself.

In the meantime… She rolled her neck, trying to massage away the tension that had gathered over hours of soothing every last wedding nerve.

At least she didn't look too much worse for wear. This silk blend she and Trella had been working on hadn't creased much at all.

Angelique stood to give a quick turn this way and that in the freestanding mirror in the corner of her office. Her black pants fell flawlessly and the light jacket with its embroidered edges fluttered with her movement while her silver cami reflected light into her face. Her makeup was holding up and only her chignon was coming apart.

She quickly pulled the pins out of her hair and gave it a quick finger-comb so her brunette tresses fell in loose waves around her shoulders. *Too* casual?

Her door guard knocked and she didn't have time to redo her hair. She moved to open the door herself.

And felt the impact like she'd stepped under a midnight sky, but one lit by stars and northern lights and the glow of a moon bigger and hotter than the sun could ever hope to be.

Angelique was dazzled and had to work not to show it, but honestly, the prince was utterly spectacular. Dark, liquid eyes that seemed almost black they were such a deep brown. Flawless bone structure with his straight nose and perfectly balanced jawline. His mouth— That bottom lip was positively erotic.

The rest of him was cool and diamond sharp. His country was renowned for being ultraconservative, but his head was uncovered, his black hair shorn into a neat business cut. He wore a perfectly tailored Western suit over what her practiced eye gauged to be an athletically balanced physique.

She swallowed. *Find a brain, Angelique.*

"Your Highness. Angelique Sauveterre. Welcome. Please come in."

She didn't offer to shake, which would have been a faux pas for a woman in Zhamair.

He did hold out his hand, which was a slight overstep for a man to demand of a woman here in Paris.

She acquiesced and felt a tiny jolt run through her as he closed his strong hand over her narrow one. Heat bloomed under her cheekbones, something his quick gaze seemed to note—which only increased her warmth. She hated being obvious.

"Hello." Not *Thank you for seeing me*, or *Call me Kasim.*

"Thank you, Maurice," she murmured to dismiss her guard, and had to clear her throat. "We'll be fine."

She was exceedingly cautious about being alone with men, or women for that matter, whom she didn't know, but the connection through Hasna and Sadiq made the prince a fairly safe bet. If a man in the prince's position was planning something nefarious, then the whole world was on its ear and she didn't stand a chance anyway.

Plus, she always had the panic button on her pendant. She almost felt like she was panicking now. Her heart rate had elevated and her stomach was in knots. Her entire body was on all-stations alert. She'd been feeling drained a few seconds ago, but one profound handshake later she was feeling energized yet oddly defenseless.

She was nervous as a schoolgirl, really, which wasn't like her at all. With two very headstrong brothers, she had learned how to hold her own against strong masculine energy.

She'd never encountered anything like this, though. Closing herself into her office with him felt dangerous. Not the type of danger she'd been trained to avoid, but inner peril. Like when she poured her soul into a piece then held her breath as it was paraded down the catwalk for judgment.

"Please have a seat," she invited, indicating the conversation area below the mural. There were no pretty views of actual Paris in this windowless room, but the office was still one of her favorite places for its ability to lock out the world. She spent a lot of time on her side of its twin desks and drafting tables.

Trella's side was empty. She was home in Spain, but they often worked here in companionable silence.

"I just made fresh coffee. Would you like a cup?"

"I won't stay long."

That ought to be good news. She was reacting way too strongly to him, but she found herself disappointed. So strange! She took such care to put mental distance between herself and others. The entire world would have this effect on her if she didn't, but he only had to glance around her private space and she felt naked and exposed. *Seen*. And she found herself longing for his approval.

He didn't seem to want to sit, so she pressed flat hands that tremored on the back of the chair she usually used when visiting with clients. "Was there something particular about the wedding arrangements you wanted to discuss?"

"Just that you should send your bill to me." He moved to set a card on the edge of Trella's desk.

She turned to follow his movement behind her. So economical and fascinating. And who was his tailor? That suit was pure artistry, the man so obviously yang to her yin.

He caught her staring.

She tucked her hair behind her ear to disguise her blush.

"Her Majesty made the same offer and you needn't have troubled yourself. It's a wedding gift for Sadiq and the princess."

He noted the familiarity of her using Sadiq's first name with a small shift of his head. "So Hasna said. I would prefer to pay."

His gaze was direct enough to feel confrontational, instantly amplifying this conversation into one of conflict. Her pulse gave a reflexive zing.

Why would he be so adamant—?

Oh, dear God! He didn't think she and Sadiq were involved, did he?

Why wouldn't he? According to the headlines, she'd slept with half of Europe. When she wasn't doing drugs or having catfights with her models, of course.

"Sadiq is a longtime friend of the family." She retreated behind the cool mask she showed the world, ridiculously crushed that he would believe those awful summations of her character. "This is something we want to do for him."

"We." His gaze narrowed.

"Yes." She didn't bring up her sister or what her family owed Sadiq for Trella's return to them. The fact that Sadiq had never once sought any glory for his heroism was exactly why he was such a cherished friend. "If that was all…" She deliberately presumed she'd had the last word on the topic. "I should get back to the final arrangements for your sister's things."

Kasim had to applaud his future brother-in-law's taste. Angelique Sauveterre had grown from a very sweet-looking girl into a stunning young woman. In person, she had an even more compelling glow of beauty.

Her long brunette hair glimmered and shifted in a rippling curtain and what had seemed like unremarkable gray eyes online were actually a mesmerizing greenish hazel. She was tall and slender, built like a model despite being the one to dress them, and her skin held a golden tone that must be her mother's Spanish ancestry.

Cameras rarely caught her with a smile on her face and when they did, it was a faint Mona Lisa slant that allowed her to live up to the reputation of her father's French blood: aloof and indifferent.

She wore that look now, but when she had first greeted him, she had smiled openly. Her beauty was so appealing, Kasim had forgotten for a moment why he was here and had been overcome with a desire to pursue her.

Perhaps this captivating quality was the reason Sadiq was so smitten?

"About those arrangements… Today went well?" He had understood it to be the final fitting of his sister's wedding gown and the bridesmaids' dresses as well as a private showing of other clothes made for Hasna, all taking place on the runway level of this building. Once the last nips and tucks were completed, the entire works would be packaged up and shipped to Zhamair for the wedding next month.

"You would have to check with the women who were here, but they all seemed pleased by the time they left." So haughty and quick to keep the focus on his sister.

From what he'd heard around his penthouse, the consensus had been a high level of ecstasy with everything from the clothes to the imported cordial to the finger sandwiches and pastries.

"Hasna doesn't seem to have any complaints," he downplayed. "Which is why I'm willing to spare her the nuisance of replacing all that you've promised her."

Angelique was tall in her heels. Not as tall as him, but taller than most women he knew, and she grew taller at his words, spine stiffening while her eyelashes batted once, twice, three times. Like she was filtering through various responses.

"All that we've *made* for her," she corrected, using a light tone, but it was the lightness of a rapier. Pointed and dangerous. "Why on earth would you refuse to let her have it?"

"You can drop the indignation," he advised. "I'm not judging. I've had mistresses. There is a time to let them go and yours has arrived."

"You think I'm Sadiq's mistress. And that as his *mistress*, I offered to make his bride's gown and trousseau. That's a rather generous act for a *mistress*, isn't it?"

She repeatedly spat the word as if she was deeply offended.

He pushed his hands into his pants pockets, rocking back on his heels.

"It's a generous act to arrange a private showing for such a large party at a world-famous and highly exclusive Paris design house." It hadn't been only his mother and sister, but Sadiq's mother and sisters, along with cousins and friends from both sides.

The cost of something like today wasn't so high as to imperil his riches, of course. The groom's family could equally afford it and given the extent of the Sauveterre wealth, and the rumors that the family corporation had underwritten this folly of an art project in the first place, he imagined Angelique wouldn't be too far out of pocket, either.

"Had this afternoon been the only line item offered at no charge, I wouldn't have batted an eye," he said. "But the gown? I know my sister's taste." He imagined it had easily run to six figures. "And to throw in wedding costumes for the rest of the party? Including mothers of the bride *and* groom?"

"Sadiq's parents and sisters are also friends of the family."

"Plus a full wardrobe for Hasna to begin her married life," he completed with disbelief. "All at no cost? This is more than a 'gift' from a 'family friend.' If I had learned of it sooner, I would have taken steps long before today."

Hasna had been chattering nonstop about her big day, but what did he care about the finer details? He was glad she was marrying for love, he wanted everything to go well for her, but the minutia of decor and food and colors to be worn had meant nothing to him. It wasn't until he had noted she was grossly under budget—not like her at all—that he had quizzed her on when to expect an invoice for the dress.

"If I'm Sadiq's mistress, then I should want the fat commission off this! I would have told him to *make* his bride come to us as a payoff for losing his support—

which I don't need, by the way." The hiss in her tone sliced the air like a blade. "That is *not* the way it went at all. Hasna didn't even know Sadiq knew us. She said we were her dream designer and he arranged it secretly, to surprise her. *We're* the ones who decided not to charge him."

"Yes, funny that he would have kept this tremendously close 'friendship'—" he let her hear his disdain "—such a secret from the woman he had been courting for a year and professed to love. I might have understood if he *was* paying you off." He wouldn't have condoned it, not when Hasna had fought so hard for a love match and had managed to convince him that Sadiq returned her feelings, but at least he would have seen the why of this ridiculous arrangement.

"Have you discussed this with Sadiq?" she demanded frostily, arms crossed. "Because I am as insulted on his behalf as I am on my own."

"Sadiq is plainly not capable of doing what is needed. I will advise him after the fact."

"I am not sleeping with Sadiq! I don't sleep with married men, or engaged ones, either."

"I'm fairly confident you stopped sleeping with him once the engagement was announced. I can account for his whereabouts since then."

"He knows you're watching him like that? With these awful suspicions about him?"

"I don't judge him for having lovers prior to settling down. We all do it."

Although it annoyed him that his brother-in-law had slept with this particular woman. Kasim didn't examine too closely why that grated. Or wonder too much about how such a soft-spoken man had managed to seduce her. Sadiq had always struck Kasim as being more book-smart than street-smart, earnest and studious and almost as naive as Hasna.

This woman was surprisingly spirited. She would dominate someone like Sadiq.

Which more than explained why Sadiq hadn't been able to end things as definitively as he should.

"And I'm…what?" she prodded. "Trying to coax him back by outfitting his wife? Your logic is flawed, Your Highness."

Her impertinence took him aback, it was so uncommon in his life. The most sass he heard from anyone was from his sister and she typically confined it to light teasing, never anything with this much bite.

He found Angelique's impudence both stimulating and trying. She obviously didn't understand who she was dealing with.

"Why are you arguing? I'm offering to *pay* you for the work you've done. The more you resist admitting the truth and promising not to see him again, the more likely I am to lose patience and pull the plug on this entire arrangement, Hasna's tears be damned."

"You would do that?" Her jaw slacked with disbelief. "To your sister?"

She had no idea to what lengths he would go—had gone—to protect his family.

He wouldn't allow himself to be drawn into yet another inner debate about his actions on that score. It still wrenched his heart, especially when Hasna still cried so often, but he had done what he had to. Ruthlessly.

And would do it again.

But he would not see his sister's heart broken again. She loved Sadiq and Sadiq would be the faithful husband she desired him to be. If that meant fast-tracking a new wedding gown, so be it.

He let Angelique read his resolve in his silence.

She stood there with her chin lifted in confrontation, trying very hard to look down her nose at him. "All I have to do is say that I'm Sadiq's mistress and this goes away?"

"Plus send me the bill and never contact Sadiq again."

"I can give your money to charity," she pointed out.

"You can. The important thing is that you will not be able to hold the debt over Sadiq's head."

"Ah, finally I learn my real motivation." Her arms came out in amazement. "I was beginning to think I was the stupidest mistress alive."

"Oh, I'm quite in admiration of your cleverness, Angelique."

His use of her name made her heart, which was already racing at this altercation, take a jump and spin before landing hard.

"Have we arrived at first names, Kasim?" It was a deliberate lob back, not unlike when she played tennis with her siblings and she was so well matched she had to throw everything she had into each swing of her racket.

This man! She had spent years developing a shield against the world and he brushed it aside like it was a cobweb, making her react from a subterranean level. It was completely unnerving.

His lashes flinched at her use of his given name. *Good.*

"Your insolence toward me is unprecedented. Take extreme care, *Angelique*."

Her fingernails were digging into her own upper arms, she was so beside herself. She used the sharp sting to keep a cool head. She had training for this type of negotiation, she reminded herself. He thought he was holding a small fortune in seed pearls and silk hostage, but he was actually holding a knife to the throat of her sister's happiness along with the debt their family owed to Sadiq.

Given that, there was no way Angelique wanted to jeopardize the wedding arrangements or cause a long-term rift.

Listen. That was the first step, she reminded herself as her ears pounded with her racing pulse. Apparently Kasim felt he wasn't being heard.

"To be clear," she said with forced calm, "you believe I've orchestrated this to put Sadiq into my debt?"

"Perhaps not financially. His family is wealthy in resources and political standing as well as actual gold. You've managed to neutralize yourself in my sister's eyes, so she couldn't possibly see you as a threat if you were to move in at a later date for whatever Sadiq was deemed useful for."

"Can I ask how you concluded that I'm so cold-blooded? Because even the online trolls don't accuse me of this sort of thing." She was nice! Her family regularly told her she was *too* nice.

"If your heart was involved, you would have refused this commission altogether. If you wanted to retaliate for a broken heart, you wouldn't be trying so hard to please Hasna. No. I've told you, I've had mistresses. I understand exceedingly practical women. This is an investment in your future. I accept that on a philosophical level, but not when it risks my sister's happiness. That I cannot allow. So." He nodded decisively at the card he'd left on the desk. "Send me the bill. Do not contact him again."

He made as if to leave.

"Wait!" She leaped forward and grabbed his arm.

He froze, gaze locking onto her hand on his sleeve for one powerful heartbeat before he lifted his eyes. His face was filled outrage and something else, something glittering and fiercely masculine.

"Have we arrived at *that* level of familiarity, Angelique?" He pivoted in a swift move to face her, taking her own arm in his opposite grip.

It was the sudden dive and snatch of a predatory bird catching prey in its talons.

They stood like that in what seemed like a slowdown in time. Her heart pounded so hard her lungs could barely inflate against it.

"We're not finished t-talking." Her voice came out painfully thin. She knew she should release him and step back, but she was quite blown away by the masculine interest that flared to life in his gaze.

She wasn't falsely modest. She knew she was beautiful. It was one of the reasons camera lenses so often turned on her. Men looked at her with desire all the time.

There was no reason she should react to *this* man's naked hunger. But she did.

A very animalistic sexual reaction pierced deep in her loins, flooding her with heat and… Yes, it was reciprocal desire. He was looking at her as if he found her appealing and she certainly found him as attractive as they came. There might even be something chemical here because her gaze dropped involuntarily to his mouth. Longing rose within her.

His lips quirked.

She knew he was reading her reaction and was amused. It stung. She felt raw and gauche. It was the bane of her existence that she couldn't always stop whatever feelings were overtaking her. This was so intense it was unprecedented, touching her at all levels. Physical, mental, emotional… He held her entire being enthralled.

"We are finished talking," he said, while his arm bent against her grip. His hand arrived at her waist, hot and sure. His other hand tightened slightly on her arm, drawing her forward a half step, commanding, but not forcing. "If you would like to start something new, however…"

Don't, she ordered herself, but it was too late. His mouth was coming down to hers and she was parting her lips in eager reception.

CHAPTER TWO

HE KNEW HOW to use that sexually explicit mouth of his, firmly capturing her lips in a hot, hard kiss. He slid a hand to the back of her head, rocked his damp mouth across hers, and damn well made love to her mouth like he had the absolute right!

She knew immediately that he was punishing her, but not in a violent way. He wanted her response, wanted to make her melt and succumb to him, to prove his mastery of her and this situation.

And he was doing it, sliding right past her resistance, ready to make her his conquest.

Hard-learned shreds of self-protection rallied. She had trained to meet any attack with an attack of her own.

She kissed him back with all the incensed outrage he had provoked in her, all the frustration that he affected her this powerfully.

She didn't accept his kiss. She matched it. She stepped into his space so the heat off his body penetrated the silk she wore, branding her skin through it. Then she scraped her teeth in a threat across his bottom lip and stabbed her own fingers into his hair. It was completely unlike her to be sexually aggressive, but how dare he come in here with his accusations and intimidations?

Did this feel like she was daunted? Did it?

She felt the surprise in him, and the hardening as he grew excited.

His reaction fed hers. The quickening of arousal in her swelled, rising like a tide that picked her off her feet, washing her in heat, sensitizing her skin and making her hyperaware of her erogenous zones. Her back arched to crush her breasts against his hard chest. Her pelvis nudged into the shape behind his fly, inciting both of them.

His arms tightened around her and he kissed her harder. Not taking control so much as pressing his foot to the accelerator so they burned hotter and faster down the track they were on. His hand slid down to her backside, possessively claiming a plump cheek through silk.

The sensation was so acutely good, the moment rushing so fast beyond her control, Angelique pulled back to release a small moan and gasp for air.

He growled and ran his mouth down her throat, now angling her hips into his so he ground himself against her with blatant intention.

She let him, completely overcome by the moment. She was used to being treated somewhere between a trophy and a revered goddess on a pedestal. No man had ever kissed her like a woman who was not just wanted, but *craved*. This was *real*.

It felt earthy and elemental.

Pure.

She let her head hang back, hair falling freely, and maybe, yes, she was succumbing, but not to him. To this. *Them*. What they were creating together.

He muttered something that sounded like an incantation and his lips moved from her collarbone to the line of her camisole.

She gasped, "Yes," aching for him to bare her breasts to his mouth, she felt so full and tight. When his hand moved up to her chest to caress along the edge—

Wait.

"Don't—" she tried to say, but he had already picked up the silver disk of her pendant to move it over her shoulder.

One second, Kasim was sunk deep in arousal, well on his way to making love with a woman of exceptional passion.

Then the door crashed open and men burst in with guns drawn.

His heart exploded.

He instinctively tried to shove Angelique behind him, but she resisted, shouting, "I'm fine! Orchid, orchid! Stand down. Orchid!"

She held out a splayed hand like it could deflect bullets and tried to scramble in front of *him*, as if she could protect him with that soft, slender figure, but Kasim was pumped with as much adrenaline as the invaders. He locked his arms protectively around her while his brain belatedly caught up to recognize that these were guards he'd seen on his way in.

"I'm fine," Angelique insisted in a shaken tone. "Stand down. Seriously," she said with a look up at Kasim that was naked and mortified. "Let me go so I can defuse this." Her hand pressed his shoulder.

Kasim's arms were banded so firmly around her, he had to consciously force himself to relax his muscles.

"I'm fine," she assured her guards as she slid away from him. She was visibly shaking. "Honestly. This was my fault. He was looking at my necklace. I should have warned him to be careful."

Looking at her necklace? Her lipstick was smudged and she was bright red from her forehead to the line of her top. Her guards weren't stupid.

They were professionals, however. One said, "Second level?"

"Water lily, and did you really?" She went across to a panel and reset something, then sighed and crossed to her desk to pick up her smartphone with a hand that still trembled. "Thank you. Please resume your stations."

The guards holstered their weapons and retreated, closing the door behind them.

While her phone rang with the video call she'd placed, she plucked a tissue and leaned into a small desk mirror to hurriedly wipe her mouth. "This will only take a sec, but if I don't—"

A male voice barked a gruff *"Oui."*

"*Bonjour*, Henri." Angelique tilted the phone so she could see the screen. She still looked somewhere between dumbfounded and grossly embarrassed, but was trying to paste a brave smile over it.

Kasim was utterly poleaxed. That kiss had been so intensely pleasurable, all he could think about was continuing from where they'd left off. *Get off the phone.*

"*Je m'excuse*. Totally my fault," Angelique continued. "False alarm. Orchid, orchid. It was only a drill."

"Qu'est ce qui c'est passé?"

"Long story and I'm in the middle of something. Can I call you later?"

"I'm looking at the security records."

Angelique closed her eyes in a small wince. "Yes," she said in a beleaguered tone, as though answering an unasked question. "The prince is still here. May I *please* call you later?"

"One hour," he directed and they ended the call.

Angelique dropped the phone onto her desktop and let out an exasperated breath.

"Ramon will be next. My other brother," she provided, nodding as her phone dinged. "There he is. Spanish Inquisition." She clasped her hands and looked to the ceiling with mock delight. "So fun! *Thanks.*"

"You're blaming me?" He hadn't thought he could be more astonished by all that had just happened.

She shrugged as she acknowledged the text, then dropped the phone again.

Moving to the shelf in the corner, she said, "How about that coffee?"

Angelique moved to where the French press had been sitting so long it bordered on tepid. She shakily pushed down the plunger and poured two short cups, needing something to calm her nerves.

Yes, let's not cause a rift with the wedding, Angelique, by having the Prince of Zhamair shot dead in your office.

What had happened to her that she'd let him kiss her like that? From the moment he'd walked in here, he'd been tapping a chisel into her. Now she was fully cracked open, all of her usual defenses and tricks of misdirection useless. It took everything she had not to let him see how thoroughly he'd thrown her off her game.

"Cream and sugar?" she asked, buying time before she had to turn around.

"Black."

She finished pouring and made herself face him.

He paused in using his handkerchief to check for traces of her lipstick against his mouth and tucked it away. He looked positively unruffled as he took one cup and saucer from her, his steady grip cutting the clatter of china down by half.

She quickly picked her own cup off its saucer and took a bolstering sip of the one she'd doctored into a syrupy milk shake.

The silence thickened.

She tried to think of something to say, but her mind raced to make sense of their kiss. What had he meant about starting something new? What did he even think of her now? Her level of security on its best days had suitors running for the hills.

He wasn't a suitor, she reminded herself. He was an arrogant dictator who had his wires crossed. That's why she'd grabbed his arm. She hadn't been able to let him leave thinking the worst. *Demanding* the worst.

"I wondered about the gauntlet of security I had to run in order to get in here," he said, eyeing her thoughtfully. "I didn't realize this was still such an issue for your family."

Yes, let's talk about my sister's kidnapping and how it continues to affect all of us. Her favorite topic.

"We're very vigilant about keeping it a nonissue. As you witnessed." She was trying to forget how horrifying it had been to have her guards interrupt the best kiss of her life because she'd been too dazed by it to prevent a rookie error with the panic button.

But she supposed the kidnapping was the reason this meeting had come about, ever rippling from the past into the future, so... Very well. There were days they revisited that dark time and this was one of them.

As she made that decision, she was able to move behind her desk and set her coffee aside with a modicum of control. Flicking her gaze, she invited him to take a chair.

"I'll stand."

"Suit yourself. Either way I know I've captured your full attention." She clasped her hands on her desktop, trying to steady herself. "I mean that literally. You won't be allowed to leave until I say you may."

He snorted, but she could see she did, indeed, have his full attention. She felt the heat of his gaze like the sun at the equator.

She swallowed. Good thing she was still wearing her pendant. Too bad he knew about it. She resisted the urge to grasp it for reassurance.

"The advantage that you continue to possess," she said, trying to mollify him, "is that you're willing to refuse the clothes we've made for your sister. I've heard all you said about wanting to protect her. I feel the same toward my own sister."

Empathy. Step two of a hostage negotiation. This was good practice, she told herself. Another drill.

"You're obviously aware of the general details of Trella's kidnapping." She had to swallow to ease how quickly those words tightened her throat. Her knuckles gleamed like polished bone buttons, but she couldn't make her hands relax.

"I know what was on the news at the time, yes."

She glanced at him, not sure what she expected to see. Avarice, maybe. People always wanted gruesome details beyond the basics of a nine-year-old girl being set up by a math tutor as boarding school was letting out, held for five days and found by police before money changed hands. There'd been more than one probing question today from different women in Hasna's bridal party.

Angelique was adept at dodging those inquiries, but they rubbed like salt in a cut every single time.

Kasim was next to impossible to read, but there was

an air of patience in him, like he understood this wasn't easy for her and was willing to wait.

Great. Now her eyes began to sting. She was a crier, unfortunately. She already knew there would be tears later, when she spoke to her brothers. It wasn't because she was upset by the false alarm, just that when a roller coaster like today happened, she tended to fall apart at some point as a sort of release.

She pushed the Remind Me Later button on her breakdown and strained her back to a posture she thought might snap her in two, but was enough to keep her composure in place.

"What's never been made public is Sadiq's part in helping us retrieve Trella."

Kasim set his cup into its saucer and placed it on the corner of her desk. Folded his arms. "Go on."

"You can't simply accept that this is the reason we feel a debt to him?"

"Your brother could give him shares in Sauveterre International, if that was the case. Your other one, the one who races, could buy him a car. Why this?"

"Sadiq is very modest. He has refused all the different times we've tried to offer any sort of compensation. He doesn't brag about his connection to our family. In every way he can, he protects our privacy. That's why we love him."

She took another brief sip of her overly sweetened coffee, trying to find the right words.

"As you've pointed out, his family has plenty of money. Gifting him shares would be…a gesture, not something meaningful. He's not the least bit into cars the way Ramon is, but when your sister mentioned she was going to approach us about making her gown, Sadiq was excited that he had an in."

Maison des Jumeaux wasn't exclusive because it was expensive—although it was obscenely so. No, their clothes were coveted because she and Trella were extremely selective about the clients they took on, always protecting their own privacy first. Gossipy socialites didn't even get an appointment, let alone an original ball gown with a hand-sewn signature label.

"Sadiq only prevailed on our friendship to ask that we accept her as a client, but of course we wanted to do it and of course we wouldn't charge him. He *wanted* to pay. I think the only reason he's letting us get away with not charging is because it's really Hasna who benefits, not him. For Trella, it's a way to repay Sadiq *herself.* It's very important to all of us, for her sake, that she be allowed to do that."

It was part of her sister's healing process. Attending the wedding had become a goal Trella was determined to achieve, come hell or high water.

"Is your sister having an affair with him?"

"That's what you got from everything I just said? No! And neither is my mother, before you go *there.* Family money paid for the materials and Trella and I are doing the work. This isn't a buy off or an attempt to hold something over Sadiq. We're contributing to his special day in the way that makes him happiest. That's *all.*"

He pondered that with a raspy scrape of his bent fingers beneath his jaw.

"You still don't believe me?" What on earth would it *take*?

"How did he help solve the kidnapping? How old was he? Fifteen? Sixteen?" His voice was thick with skepticism. "How well did he even know your family? I understood he only went to Switzerland when he began prepping for university."

"I trust this conversation won't leave this room? Because the police asked us to keep it confidential and we always have. We never speak publicly about the kidnapping because there are many details we wish to keep private."

"Of course," he muttered testily, as though he was insulted she would question his integrity.

"You know Sadiq is a bit of a computer whiz? Well, the internet was quite young and few tools had been developed for online sleuthing. It probably wouldn't even be legal now, the kind of hacking he'd done, but who cares? We have him to thank for Trella's return. And you're right that he only knew *of* us. We weren't friends yet. He was in a few classes with my brothers, but when Trella was taken, he was on the steps beside Ramon. He saw it happen and was horrified. He wanted to help and used his own time, hours and hours I might add, to create software code that produced a lead that panned out for the police. If you want more information, you can take it up with Sadiq."

The truth was, Sadiq was a security specialist. He'd merely been a nerd with a passion at that time, but now it was his private business—literally his confidential side job that she only knew about because her family had introduced him to the man who had the contract for their own security. She didn't know if even Hasna was aware that Sadiq wrote code for Tec-Sec Industries.

"There aren't many people we trust unequivocally, but Sadiq is one of them. He didn't do us a *favor*. He saved my sister's *life*. So if he wants me to make dresses for your sister for the rest of my life, I will. Happily. Without checking with *you* first."

CHAPTER THREE

KASIM HADN'T EXPECTED her to admit outright that she had had an affair with Sadiq, but he hadn't expected an explanation like this, either. It shed an entirely different light on things. He couldn't help but believe her.

Of course, she had done her best to scramble his brain with that kiss, so he forced himself to proceed cautiously.

"I'll allow that Sadiq is what the Americans call a 'geek.' He *is* very modest and I've seen that do-good streak. He always seems sincere in his kindness toward Hasna. I can believe he would take it upon himself to help a stranger's family. But I will check this with him," he warned.

"Be my guest!"

Sadiq would back her story regardless. It was a far more tasteful explanation than admitting he'd had an affair with her. It was more tasteful to *him*, Kasim acknowledged darkly.

"I may have to relay some of this to my parents." He was sorry now that his mother knew anything about this. She had already used the waiving of payment to stir up his father, basking in the importance of being the one to inform the king that there might be a scandal attached to their daughter's wedding. She could easily have put the wedding itself in jeopardy in her quest for her husband's attention, ever in competition with the king's consort, Fatina.

It was exhausting and, given his father's blood pressure and enlarged heart, Kasim expected his mother to show more sense. It was almost as if she was *trying* to provoke a heart attack. Maybe she was. Hell hath no fury, as the saying went, but at least he could defuse her latest damage with this information.

"If that's what it takes to keep both our sisters from suffering profound disappointment, fine," Angelique said stiffly, rising. "I trust they will also keep that information confidential."

"They will," he promised, brushing aside politics at home as he realized she was trying to kick him out.

He wasn't ready to leave.

His mind had barely left their kiss. The way she had responded like a boxer coming into a ring had been exhilarating.

"Have dinner with me," he said.

"Pah! Are you serious?" She blinked her mossy eyes at him. *"Why?"*

It was a completely singular reaction. Women cozied up to him and *begged* for an invitation to dine with him.

"We have more to talk about."

"Like?"

He dropped his gaze to the pink-stained tissue crumpled on her desk.

She blushed, but it wasn't all embarrassment. There was memory there, too. One that made her flush into her chest. The knowledge she was growing aroused again stimulated all the latent signals of his own desire.

Angelique looked away. "That was a mistake."

"It was an effective distraction," he allowed.

Her gaze flashed back to his. "That was *not* what I was trying to do."

He shrugged. "Nevertheless, it put certain possibilities on the table." He was already imagining that same explosive passion colliding on silk sheets. Or this desk she stood behind.

"I can't," she dismissed crisply.

"Why not?" A thought struck. "Are you in a relationship?" He tensed, dismayed.

"I wouldn't have kissed you if I was, would I?"

"I don't know." He relaxed, starting to enjoy that pique of hers. It put a pretty glow in her eyes and revealed the intoxicating passion he'd tasted on her lips. "This is why we should have dinner. So we can get to know one another."

"Are *you* in a relationship?" she shot back.

"No." He scowled, not used to anyone asking questions so direct and personal.

She relaxed slightly, but her brow quickly crinkled in consternation. "Do you want to talk more about Sadiq? You still don't believe me?"

"I want to go on a date, Angelique. I would think that was obvious."

"A *date*."

How could that take her aback? She actually retreated a half step. Her brows gave a surprised twitch, then, oddly, she looked uncertain. She dropped her gaze to her desktop. Bashful?

"I rarely date."

"Then it should be a treat to have dinner with me."

She laughed, which might have been offensive if she didn't have such a pretty, engaging laugh. Her enjoyment was genuine and thorough. At his expense.

"I won't apologize." She held up a hand as she noted the way he folded his arms and set his teeth. "It wasn't your conceit that got to me so much as the painful truth of that remark. You have no idea."

Conceit? He'd been stating a fact.

She ran a fingertip beneath her eye, smile lingering.

"In gratitude for that exceptionally good chuckle, I'll spare you some pain. I attract a lot of attention. I'm really not worth the trouble to take out. I know this because I've been told so more than once." Her amusement faded to something more sincere. Resigned. Maybe even a tad wistful and hurt.

He started to say they could dine alone at his penthouse, then recalled his Paris residence was overrun by his mother and sisters and assorted female relatives.

"Your place then," he said.

She shook her head, but there seemed to be some regret there. "Trella counts on certain spaces being kept private and our flat here is one of them."

That devotion to her sister kept getting to him. The second nature of it. He understood it very well and had to like her for it.

"Dining in public it is, then."

She grew very grave. "I'm serious, Kasim. My sort of notoriety is a punishment. You would be tarred as my lover overnight."

"Since I intend to spend the night with you, where is the harm?"

"Do you?" she scoffed, flushing with indignation. And stirred sensuality.

He saw the deepening of her color and the swirl of speculation behind her gaze. The way she swallowed and licked her lips. Her nipples rose against the light silk of her top and filmy jacket.

He smiled with anticipation.

"That's rather overconfident, isn't it?" she said snippily.

"Don't act surprised, Angelique." He flicked his gaze down to the breasts that had flattened against his chest, the pelvis that had pressed into the thrust of his. "We're very well matched and both intrigued to see where this could go. If you're so eager you don't want to go to dinner first, we can progress to that discovery right here and now. Provided you remove your necklace first."

Her chin was not so narrow as to be pointed, but not so round as to be girlish. It was as perfect as the rest of her. She set it into a stubborn angle and said, "Punishment it is."

She marched past him to the door.

"Maurice," she said as she swung the door open. "A card, please. I'll be dining with the prince later. Would you be kind enough to send someone to scout the restaurant of his choosing?"

She relayed the card to Kasim as he came up behind her. If he wished to be so forward, her glare spat at him, he could suffer the wrath of her *celebrité*.

He wasn't scared. His worst family secret had been painstakingly—and yes, agonizingly—buried. Reports that he had affairs with beautiful women only aided that particular cause.

"Your men can call that number with the details," Angelique said.

He pocketed the card thoughtfully. "I'll pick you up at seven."

"No need. My security will deliver me."

"So cautious." He felt the seeds of irritation forming. Perhaps he didn't care about the notoriety she provoked, but the triple-A level of security could become tiresome. "It's a test?" he guessed. If the arrangements for a simple dinner were too much for him, he was not prepared for the rest of the way she lived, she seemed to be conveying.

"It's my reality," she said with a flat smile.

He annoyed me.

That was the only reason Angelique had agreed to dinner.

Or so she told herself.

And repeated to Trella, when her sister rang through on the tablet before she'd got round to calling Henri.

"What's going on with you?" Trella demanded with a troubled frown. "I'm feeling… I don't know. Restless. Keyed up. Henri texted that your blip was a false alarm, but was it more serious?"

She and her sister didn't keep much from one another. There was no point. They read each other too well.

Not that they were psychic. Angelique never feared Trella could peer into her private moments, but they had an uncanny connection. Despite whatever distance might separate them, they were eerily aware of the other's emotional temperature. They *knew* if the other was happy or sad, angry or scared.

It was one of the reasons Angelique was encouraged to believe Trella was actually getting better this time. The Sauveterres were all paranoid to a point, but for Trella, terror had become her constant companion and a very debilitating one. She didn't *want* to fall apart with anxiety attacks, but for years they had struck without mercy and Angelique had always been aware when they did. It hadn't helped her own sensitive nature one little bit.

Living a cloistered life had leveled out the worst of Trella's episodes, but now she was trying to over-come her fear of being in public so she could go to Sadiq's wedding. It wasn't so much fear of actually being around people or in the public eye that held her back, but fear that any change in her routine would trig-ger fresh attacks. So it was proving to be a "two steps forward, one back" process, but she was getting there.

Angelique was just as worried that anything could cause Trella to backslide, so she was very firm in stat-ing, "Today was me being an idiot. That's *all*."

She didn't go into detail about the kiss, but gave Trella a good laugh describing the scene as Kasim set off her panic button.

"He said it would be a treat to have dinner with him. I'll show him a treat," she muttered.

"It's been a long time since you went on a date. Even longer since it was someone you were genuinely at-tracted to," Trella noted.

There went any attempt at disguising from her sister how deeply Kasim affected her.

"I don't know why I am! He's not my usual type at all."

"You don't have a type. You go out with men who make you feel guilty if you turn them down, or sorry for them."

"Well, there's no feeling sorry for this one. He's…" *Indescribable.* She was reacting to him from a com-pletely different place than she'd ever experienced. He didn't pluck her heartstrings as Trella suggested, or tweak her conscience. It was a way deeper reaction than that. He drew her to him.

And made her feel too transparent just thinking about him. She quickly mentioned she still owed Henri a call, but lingered to ask Trella, "Have you noticed… Is something going on with Henri and Cinnia?"

Trella tilted her head in consideration. "He hasn't said anything to me, but now that you say it…"

Henri didn't peep a word about anything unless he wanted it known, but if he did confide a secret, it was to Trella first. They were all close, but they each had their own special relationship with each other. It went all the way back to the day Angelique and Trella were born. Their twin brothers had been allowed to name their sisters and it had created a sense of responsibility in each boy for "his" baby sister.

Ownership, Trella and Angelique had often called it in a mutter to each other. Half the time the boys acted like their sisters were kittens picked up from the animal shelter, but it was a dynamic that had colored their entire lives. They all loved each other equally, but when it had come to holding a sister's hand or pushing her on a swing, they had naturally divided into Henri and Trella, Ramon and Angelique. Oldest with youngest, middle with middle.

Which wasn't to say that Henri was any less protective of Angelique than he was of Trella, or that Ramon was more. Trella's kidnapping had sent the boys' instincts off the scale. Their father's death six years later, when the men were barely twenty-one, had added yet another layer to their self-imposed yokes of responsibility.

Thus both men would insist on an explanation for today's false alarm.

Angelique hung up on her sister and placed the call to both brothers at once, opening with, "I can't talk long. I have a date."

Their identical faces stared back at her, Henri in the

London flat that he often shared with Cinnia, Ramon in the corporate office in Madrid. They both gave her their full attention, but Henri's expression was marginally more severe, Ramon's a shade amused.

"Do you really expect us to believe the 'looking at your necklace' story?" Ramon asked.

"Do you really want a different one?" she challenged.

"Soyez prudent, Gili,*"* Henri said. "He doesn't keep his women long and he has publicly stated that his father will choose his bride—a traditional virgin from Zhamair, no doubt. I wouldn't recommend a romance."

"Hear that, Ramon? Don't get your hopes up."

No smile out of Henri. He really was a grump these days. Angelique scanned behind him for Cinnia. She usually dipped into the screen for at least a quick hello.

"I have to go to Beijing for a week, but I'll be back in Paris after that. You can explain properly then," Henri stated.

Good luck, she thought, suppressing a snort, and took note of how permanent that sounded. *Back in Paris after that.* Henri usually divided his time between Paris and London with occasional popovers to New York and Montreal. More often than not he said "we," meaning him and his companion of two years, Cinnia.

Ramon only introduced his lovers to the family if they happened to bump into each other at a public event. Women were a catch and release sport for him and he was forever on the run anyway, covering Spain, Portugal and all of South America for Sauveterre International. The men were actively working on acquisitions in Asia and Australia, but as Ramon sometimes joked, "We're only one person."

"Trella told me not to bring her tomorrow," Ramon

said abruptly, dark brows pulling into a frown. "Did she tell you that?"

"What? No!" Angelique was taken aback. "I just spoke to her. She said, 'See you tomorrow.' We're going to finish Hasna's gown and start packing everything." Had she blocked her sister from airing some misgivings, too focused on herself and her date with Kasim?

"No, I mean she said she wants to travel to Paris alone. With guards, of course, but she doesn't want me to come with her." Ramon scratched his eyebrow. "It started because I said I was heading to Rio right after and that I had to be there until Sadiq's wedding. She said I shouldn't have to double back and she would go to Paris alone."

"Go with her anyway," Henri ordered. "I'll change my schedule and come get her, if you don't have time. Where is Mama?"

"No!" Angelique interjected. "Boys." They were thirty, but sometimes calling them that was the only way to pull them out of their patriarchal tailspins. "We've always said that Trella has to be allowed to do things in her own time. That meant not pushing before she was ready, but it also means not holding her back when she *is* ready. You know how hard she's trying."

"Exactly why she shouldn't push herself and trigger something. No. I don't like it," Henri said flatly.

"Neither do I," Ramon said.

"Too. *Bad*," Angelique said, even though her own heart was skipping and fluttering with concern for her sister. "I'll be here," she reminded. "It's a couple of hours on the private jet. I do the trip all the time."

"It's different," Ramon grumbled. "You know that."

"Let her do this," Angelique insisted, ignoring the sweat in her palms as she clutched her tight fists. "I'll text her so she knows I can come get her if she changes her mind."

She signed off with warm regards to both her brothers and finished getting ready for her date.

Angelique had to give Kasim credit. He did his homework—or his people did.

He chose a restaurant she and her family frequented for its excellent food and location atop the Makricosta, one of Paris's most luxurious hotels. The staff was also adept at protecting her privacy, not forcing her to walk through the lobby, but willing to arrange an escort from the underground parking through the service elevator.

It always amused her that the most exclusive guests of fine establishments wound up seeing plain Jane lifts and overly bright hallways cluttered with linen carts and racks of dirty food trays.

To her surprise, Kasim was in the elevator when it opened. That instantly sent its ambiance skyrocketing. He was casually elegant in a tailored jacket over a black shirt that was open at the throat.

Her blood surged, filling her with heat. What *was* it about this man?

"I didn't realize you were staying here," she said, trying not to betray his effect on her as she and Maurice stepped in.

"I wasn't. Until I had a date with you." His gaze snared hers and held it.

A jolt of excitement went through her as the suggestiveness in his comment penetrated. *Don't act surprised. We're very well matched...*

She'd never progressed so fast with a man that she'd contemplated sex on a first date. In fact, her advancement to the stage of sharing a bed was so slow, she had only got there a couple of times. Each time she had arrived with great expectation and left with marginal levels of satisfaction.

Now her mind couldn't help straying into sensual curiosity. What would it be like to sleep with Kasim? Their kiss had been very promising. She grew edgy just thinking of it.

"In case you wished to dine unseen," he added almost as an afterthought, with an idle glance at the ever stone-faced Maurice, but with a hint of droll humor deepening the corners of his sex god mouth, like he knew where her mind had gone and was laughing at her for it.

Wicked, impossible man. He had *made* her think about sleeping with him. Deliberately.

She didn't let on that his trick had worked, although her pink cheeks probably gave her away. "The restaurant is fine. I'm rarely bothered there."

The maître d' greeted her warmly by name and assured Kasim it was an honor to serve him. He showed them to a table at a window where a decorative screen had been erected prior to their arrival, enclosing them in a semiprivate alcove.

Kasim held her chair and glanced at the screen as he seated himself. "Apparently we dine unseen regardless."

"Did you want to be seen with me? You wouldn't be the first."

"I wouldn't be ashamed," he said drily. "You're very beautiful. But if you're more comfortable like this, by all means."

Angelique tried not to bask in the compliment as their drink orders were taken. She had freshened her makeup and vetted her outfit over the tablet with Trella, settling on an ivory cocktail dress with a drop waist that ended above her knees in a light flare. The sleeves were overlong and held a belled cuff while the entire concoction was embellished with some of Trella's best work in seed pearls and silver beads.

Public appearances were always this fine balancing act between avoiding being noticed but wanting to show Maison des Jumeaux in its best light if she happened to be photographed, all while trying not to look over-or underdressed for the actual event.

"Judging by what you said today, I didn't think there'd been recent threats. Is this just the vigilance against them that you spoke of?" He nodded at the screen.

"That's me trying to maintain some level of mystery," she joked, but her voice was flat. "Yet another reason I don't bother dating," she expanded. "You already know far more about me than I do about you...not that whatever you've read online is true." She *so* hoped he knew that and wondered why it mattered so much.

"You haven't stalked me?" His brows angled with skepticism. "Asked Hasna about me?"

"I rarely surf at all. Too much chance of running into myself. And no. I'm too protective of my own privacy to invade someone else's." She didn't bring up that Henri had been more than happy to check him out on her behalf. "In my months of working with your sister, she only volunteered the information that you insisted she finish school in exchange for supporting her desire for a love marriage and that you refuse to sing at the wedding, even though your voice is quite good."

He snorted. "It's not. And she's lucky our father is allowing any music at all, let alone a handful of Western tunes. That's it?"

She debated briefly, then admitted quietly, "She told

me you lost your brother a few years ago. I'm very sorry." At least her sister was alive. She was grateful for that every single day.

Kasim looked away to the window as though absorbing a slap.

"I shouldn't have brought it up," she murmured.

"It's public knowledge," he dismissed, bringing his attention back to her with his thoughts and feelings well hidden.

She instantly felt like a hypocrite for claiming she didn't invade others' privacy. She desperately wanted to know what he was thinking behind that stony mask. He fascinated her. That was why she had come to dinner. There. She'd admitted it to herself. She wanted to know more about him.

"It seems I do have the advantage." He shot his cuff as he leaned back to regard her. "In my defense, even the weather and financial pages have click-bait links with your name in them. I can't help but see whichever headline is making the rounds."

"Which is why I look out the window to see if I need an umbrella and ask my doorman for the news. Thank you," she murmured as their wine was poured.

When they were alone, he said, "The story was very compelling. I was about your brothers' age. Hasna was yours. I couldn't help feeling invested in the outcome. I suppose the entire world presumed it gave them a stake in your lives."

The world had presumed a stake in their lives long before her sister was kidnapped. It was one of the reasons her family had been targeted.

She didn't bother lamenting it aloud. Her family had learned to accept what couldn't be changed. Identical twin boys born to a French tycoon and his Spanish aristocrat wife had been fairly unremarkable, but when a pair of identical girls had come along six years later, and the four together had won the genetic lottery on good looks, well, the children had become media darlings without being consulted. She had never been Angelique. She was "one of The Sauveterre Twins."

Which she would never for a moment wish to change. She adored her siblings and wore the designation with pride. It was the attention they relentlessly attracted that exhausted her.

"It's been fifteen years. I would have thought the fascination would have died down," she said with a self-deprecating smile.

"With your sister living in seclusion? It only adds to the mystery." He eyed her as though he wondered if it was a ploy to keep the attention at a fever pitch. "The free exposure can't be hard on business."

"You're wrong," she said bluntly, amused by the way his expression stiffened at being accused of such a thing. "Discretion is one of the most valuable services we offer our clients. The planning of a maternity gown for the red carpet, for instance, when the pregnancy won't be announced until closer to the event. Or a wedding gown when the engagement is still confidential. Sometimes the wedding itself is a secret affair. Trella and I live under such tight security it's fairly easy to extend that amenity to clients."

She sent a pithy look at the screen beside them.

"Until a tourist wants a selfie with me like I'm a historic fountain. Or a shopkeeper wants instant publicity and posts the brand of toothpaste I prefer. And yes, I know I can stay in and buy online. That's what Trella does. But I like to be human and walk in the sun, browse shops for housewares and books. Being followed and photographed while doing it is far more nuisance than benefit and just makes poor Maurice's job harder."

Kasim flicked his gaze beyond her to where she knew Maurice would have been seated at a table with a sight line on her. He was likely sipping a coffee while awaiting a light meal, gaze monitoring the restaurant's employees and patrons.

"It's the reason I don't date," she said, noting where he was looking. "Men don't care to be watched while they attempt to romance a woman."

"It would be a special predilection, wouldn't it? One I don't possess, I'll admit."

She had to chuckle at that, relieved he had a sense of humor about it.

"And if I were merely attempting something that had little chance of success, I might be self-conscious," he added, gaze clashing into hers. "But I'm not."

Oh.

"You're a very confident man." She allowed herself to lean into the fire, to let the heat of his interest warm her cheeks and glow in her eyes. "You come on very strong."

"I didn't expect to find you so intriguing." He held her gaze without actually looking into her eyes. Instead he visually caressed her face, touching her loose hair with his dark gaze. She couldn't look away as he studied her like she was a painting. "A meeting in your office would have sufficed if you'd been less... impassioned. You're not like anyone I've ever encountered."

She had expected another compliment on her looks. This was far more disarming. It made her feel like he saw within her, to the real woman inside, the one few noticed or understood. Plus it was an acknowledgment of something she'd had to work on most of her life: being unique from her sister and being comfortable with her own powerful emotions.

If she wasn't careful, she would be seduced without realizing it. He was very good at it.

"I like your sister, you know. I wouldn't want to hurt her. She's delightful." She waited a beat, deliberate with her timing as she added, "Not much like you at all."

His mouth twitched and he took a thoughtful sip of his wine. His lashes were so thick and long, they were almost pretty, but he was undeniably masculine as he lifted them to regard her. There was nothing soft in the dangerous air he projected.

She held her breath.

"Feel privileged, Angelique. I'm letting you get away with a lot."

She bit the inside of her lip, wondering if she should apologize. Was she ruining this little bit of rapport they'd arrived at?

"Hasna is a lovely person," he agreed. "And you're right. She and I are opposites. Women lead different lives in our country so they grow up with gentler personalities." Something about that statement made him briefly pensive. "At least that's what I've always thought made her so tenderhearted and me more practical and assertive."

"Now you're not so sure?" She tried to read his inscrutable expression. "Supporting her desire for a love marriage sounds rather sentimental, if you ask me."

His cheeks hollowed as though he considered his words carefully.

"She was very upset about losing Jamal. I'm not incapable of compassion. I want her to be happy in her marriage and we've established that we both wish to protect our sisters from heartache, have we not? Is that how you came to open a fashion house with yours?"

She heard that as the shift in topic it was, which intrigued her because something about the way he was trying to compensate Hasna for their brother's loss struck her as guilt. Or responsibility, maybe.

Because she was the sensitive, intuitive one. In some ways it was her burden, but she couldn't deny that she often picked up on things others missed.

"Trella started making her own clothes," she began, then recalled why. Those early years of recovery had been so brutal. As if the kidnapping hadn't been traumatic enough, the press had crucified Trella, dubbing her The Fat One among other things.

"It's not that interesting a story, actually. Just something that both of us enjoyed. We have an artistic flare and work well together so we gave it a shot."

Trella was actually The Smart One. Her business plan had been excellent. The boys would have underwritten anything she'd proposed, to spoil her and give her something she could control and succeed at, but she had been determined to make her mark on the world in a very specific way. Feminine strength imbued every aspect of Maison des Jumeaux. Angelique was deeply proud to be part of it.

"The press makes a lot of the fact that family money gave us our start, but we've paid back the initial loan. I don't know why it's important to me that you know that."

"So I don't think you're chasing Sadiq's money, presumably."

"No." She couldn't help smirking at the way he stiffened every time she contradicted him. "I think it's because I know you respect women who are ambitious and independent. Isn't that why you were so adamant Hasna finish school?"

"No." He waited out the delivery of their appetizers before expanding on his reply. "The more accurate reason is that I didn't want to give my support too quickly or easily because, in order to broker that deal with my father, I promised that my own marriage would be an arranged one. With a suitable bride from my own country, one he could choose. You understand why I'm telling you that."

CHAPTER FOUR

"THAT'S QUITE A SACRIFICE." Angelique's eyelids shimmered with golden tones, shielding her thoughts.

"It's duty. My father is not what anyone would call progressive. I have visions of a modern Zhamair. It would be good for our people, but I will never be given the chance to steer it that way if I don't play by his rules. My uncle would be more than happy to accept the crown if my father decided I was too liberal. My uncle is even more of a throwback than my father. So I have agreed to my father's condition. But I'm not in a hurry to give up my freedom."

He let himself admire her smooth skin with its warm glow, her mouth gently pouted in thought. Their kiss was still branding a permanent pattern into his memories—exactly the sort of freedom he was loathe to relinquish by tying himself down.

"You intend to be faithful to your wife, then, once you're married?"

"Certainly until heirs have been established. After that…" He scratched beneath his chin. "My father has two wives. I have not observed having more than one woman coming to your bed to be as idyllic as it sounds."

Her lashes came up, gaze curious as all Westerners were when he mentioned it. "Jealousy?" she guessed.

"How did you know?" Kasim said drily.

He privately thought the polygamy was the reason his father was so ferociously implacable, refusing to evolve with the times or even hold a rational conversation. He consistently asserted his will and slammed doors on further discussion. If he didn't control every aspect of his life with an iron fist, his wives might tear him in two.

That emotional turmoil bleeding all over his childhood was the reason Kasim had grown such a thick shield of detachment. How else could he have withstood the helpless agony of witnessing his brother's struggle? How else could he have been ruthless enough to end it? Taken altogether, it was the reason he was just as happy to marry a stranger. Love provoked madness and pain of every variety.

"Was your father's marriage to the queen an arranged one?"

"It was." He knew where she was going with that. "And it was a contented one until he brought Fatina into it. Which is why I don't intend to do anything similar."

"Because you want to rule," she murmured, gaze narrowed as she weighed that.

"That concern you feel for your sister's well-being? That's how I feel for my entire nation," he explained quietly.

He had never put it in so many words. As her lashes widened at the magnitude of what he was saying, he experienced a lurch in his heart. He had always thought of it as a goal, not a sacrifice. Suddenly he saw it differently.

"None of us are in a hurry to marry," Angelique mused, dropping her gaze again. "We're a tight bunch, my siblings and I. Letting someone into my life means opening all our lives. That demands a lot of trust and we've all been stung at least once, so we're all wary. It's why I don't even bother with affairs anymore, contrary to reports online." She flashed him an admonishing look. "Don't you dare say that if I don't have affairs, it should be a treat to spend a night with you."

"Oh, I'm starting to see the honor will be all mine." He meant it. Everything she had shared pointed to a woman who lived within her own restrictions. No wonder she had exploded in his arms. She was a powder keg of suppressed passion.

She sputtered with laughter, shaking her head. "You are an incredibly arrogant man."

"There is an expression, isn't there? About a kettle and a pot?"

"I'm not arrogant." She dismissed that with a shake of her loose hair and a haughty elevation of her chin.

"You are," he assured her. It was as captivating as the rest of her.

"No." She looked him right in the eye. "My sister is the brash one. Deep down." Her irises reflected the candlelight between them, mesmerizing as the glow of a fire in the blackest night in the desert. Tears gathered to brim her lashes. "I pretend to be."

She blinked to clear the wetness and her eyes widened with forced lightness.

"I am her and she is me. At least, that's how it feels sometimes. Can we talk about something else?"

"I wasn't talking about her. I was talking you into my bed," he pointed out, made cautious by that moment of acute vulnerability. Was it concern for her sister? Or an indication of a deeper sensitivity in her personality?

He recoiled inwardly from that. He had enough emotional drama in his life. He needed her to come to this with as light a heart as he had.

"I want *you*," he stressed. "What will that take, Angelique? Reassurances about your security? I see you've changed your necklace. Is that one rigged?" He winced as he recalled her talk of suitors having to tolerate being constantly under observation. "We're not being recorded, are we?"

"No. This one requires two hands to twist and set it off." She ran the teardrop pearl back and forth on its chain. "So I rarely wear it. In terms of physical safety, I have no concerns about being alone with you. I'm not even worried you would write a tell-all afterward."

"The sting you mentioned? A man did that to you?"

"One did. You can find him living under a false name in whichever Eastern European slum men use to hide when they've been financially ruined by defamation litigation and threatened with castration."

"Your brothers went after him?"

"*I* went after him," she said crossly. "Give me credit."

"Is that a warning? I would never do such a thing," he promised her. "I may be nonchalant about spending the night with a woman, but I don't degrade myself or my partner. You can be assured of my discretion."

Her shoulder hitched in acceptance, but she wore her Mona Lisa expression.

"You're resisting temptation. Why?"

He reached across to take her hand in his, cradling her knuckles in his palm. He used his thumb to catch at hers, pressing her hand open so he held the heel of her palm gently arched open to his touch. He smoothed his thumb to the inside of her wrist, pleased to find her pulse unsteady and fast.

"Is it because it's only one night?"

"No," she said softly. "That's actually a plus. Like I said, I don't fit others into my life very well."

"If you weren't reacting to me, I would finish our meal and send you home, but I can see your struggle against your own feelings. What's holding you back then? You clearly want to."

He caressed that sensitive area at the base of her hand, where a former lover had once told him life and fate lines had their root. *That's why it's such a sensitive place on a woman's body,* she'd said.

Angelique caught her breath.

He didn't believe in the supernatural, but he did believe in nature's ability to create sexual compatibility. That sort of gift should be relished when it was offered.

"My room is just down the hall. Anyone who sees us leave the restaurant will think we're going to the elevators."

He lifted her hand and pressed his lips into her life, into her fate, as he tasted and grew drunk with anticipation.

Oh, he was good.

Her pulse went mad under the brush of his lips and she had to concentrate to draw a breath.

"I told myself I was only coming out to prove to you I wasn't worth the trouble."

"To scare me off? I don't scare."

I do, she wanted to say. She wanted to go to his room so badly it terrified her. And she didn't understand why this want sat like a hook in the middle of her chest, pulling her toward him with a painful sting behind her breastbone. She didn't know how to handle any of this because she wasn't the bold, confident one.

What would Trella do?

It was a habitual thought, one that harked way back to her earliest years when her sister had been the one to stride eagerly forward while Angelique hung back.

She brushed aside thoughts of Trella. She shared almost everything with her twin, but not this. Not him.

That was what scared her. Who was she if not Trella's other half?

An internal tearing sensation made her touch her chest. She immediately felt the beading on her dress and wondered why she had worn Trella's creation. Armor, she supposed, but this wasn't about Trella. That was what made this situation so starkly unique and put her at such a loss.

In this moment she was only Angelique. Except she didn't know what Angelique would do in a situation like this. Her other lovers had wanted one of The Sauveterre Twins and the fame or influence or bragging rights that came with it. She had gone with them hoping for a feeling of fulfillment, but had never found it.

Kasim wanted *her*. That's what made him so irresistible.

And she had a feeling this would be more than fulfilling. Profound. Maybe life-altering.

Which was terrifying in its own way, seeing as it was only for one night, but if she refused him out of fear, she knew she would regret it for the rest of her life.

The lights were set low in the opulent suite. Champagne chilled in a bucket next to an intimately set table overlooking the Eiffel Tower. The muted notes of a French jazz trio coated the air with a sexy moan of a saxophone, subtle bass strings and a brush on a drum.

Angelique was walking into a setup and wasn't even sure how she had arrived here. It felt like she had floated. There had been a conversation with Maurice, who had escorted them down the hall. She had instructed him to go back and finish his own meal and put theirs on hold. Charles, her second guard, stood post at the door of the suite. He had assured her as she entered that he had inspected and secured these rooms prior to her arriving at the restaurant and had been at this door ever since.

They were very mundane details that were decidedly *un*romantic, but they had each been one of the many tiny steps that had carried her toward this moment.

"I am fascinated with this dress," Kasim said, picking up her hand and carrying it over her head, urging her to twirl very slowly before him. "It is a work of art. I'm afraid to touch it." He lowered her hand, but kept it in his, so they were facing one another. "But I want to touch you."

His words made her heart stutter. She tugged free of his grip and walked to an end table where she set down her pocketbook.

"I'm not used to being touched."

"I'm not going to chase you through these rooms, Angelique. If you've changed your mind, say so."

She turned to face him. "I haven't. I'm just nervous."

"Don't be. I won't rush you."

He didn't have to. She was rushing herself, not ignoring misgivings so much as refusing to give in to the natural hesitation that had held her back one way or another most of her life. If her sister hadn't pressed her toward this fashion house idea, she never would have had the nerve.

So part of her was saying, *Don't be impulsive*. But the truth was, this moment had been brewing since their kiss this afternoon.

This was why she had come to dinner with him. She was a person of deep feeling and what he made her feel was too strong to resist. She had never felt so much like herself as she did with this man.

But she wanted to be herself. She wanted him to want Angelique.

She lowered the zip on the back of her dress, slowly drawing the shoulders down her arms and very carefully stepping out of it without letting the skirt brush the floor.

Kasim's inhale was audible over the quiet music, sounding as a long, sharp hiss.

"You, however…" he said in a rasp. "Seem in a big hurry."

"You said you were afraid to touch it." Avoiding looking at him, she took great care with folding the dress in half lengthwise, then gently set it on the arm of the wingback chair.

She was naked except for her high silver shoes and a pair of lavender cheekies that cut a wide swath of lace across her hips and the top half of her buttocks. She had done enough quick changes backstage alongside half-naked models that she wasn't particularly self-conscious.

Nevertheless, it was intimidating to turn and face him. At the same time, it was a rebirth of sorts, standing there naked and vulnerable. Tears flew into her eyes at the significance of shedding the shield of her sister and being only Angelique.

Would he like her?

"What's this?" Kasim murmured, coming forward to cup her face and make her meet his gaze with her wet one.

"I don't often let myself *be*." Life was far easier when

she kept her thoughts on the future or her sister or a piece of fabric. Allowing the moment to coalesce around her, so she experienced the full spectrum of emotions he provoked—impatience and sexual yearning, uncertainty and deep attraction—it was huge and scary.

She smoothed her hand down the lapel of his suit jacket, then warily looked up at him, fearful of what she might find in his gaze.

What she saw made the ground fall away beneath her feet.

His eyes were hungry and fierce, but there was something tender there, too.

"I'll take care of you," he promised in a low growl, then dipped his head to kiss her.

She started slightly as his arms went around her and a jolt of such acute pleasure went through her it was almost like a shock of electricity.

He paused briefly, gentled his kiss. Then, as she pressed into him, encouraging him to continue, he deepened it, sweet yet powerful, making her knees weaken.

They quietly consumed one another. She speared her fingers into his hair and met his tongue with her own and let herself flow wholly into the kiss.

Releasing a jagged noise, he pulled away and threw off his jacket. Yanked at the buttons on his shirt. "Damn you for being so far ahead of me. You do this."

He left his shirt open but tucked in and set his hands on her bare waist, capturing her lips with his as he ran his hands around to her lower back, making her shiver then melt as he molded her closer. They were chest to chest, hot dry skin to hot hairy chest.

A sob of broken pleasure escaped her. More. She needed more of him, and pushed at his shirt, smoothing her hands over the powerful shape of his shoulders.

With a brief pull back, she yanked his shirt free of his pants, then they were embracing again, her hands free to steal beneath the hanging tails of his shirt to caress the warmth of his flexing back.

Skin. Lips. A cold belt buckle against her bare stomach and a hard shape behind his fly that made her both nervous and excited. She had never abandoned herself to desire, had never allowed herself to be so vulnerable, but she didn't have a choice. Time stopped. All she knew was the feel of him stroking her skin, pressing her closer, fondling her breast then looking at where her nipple stabbed at his palm.

He bent and covered the tight bead with his hot mouth, tongue playing in a way that had her shuddering as ripples of pure delight went straight down her middle to pool in her loins. When he moved to the other one, she ran her hands through his hair, loving the feel of the soft spiky strands between her fingers, and spoke his name like an endearment.

A moment later, he dropped to his knees, taking her underpants as he went and leaving them twisted on her shoes as he stroked his hands up and down her thighs, gaze so hot on the flesh he had bared that she felt it. Her inner muscles tightened and a press of moisture wet her lower lips in anticipation.

She closed her eyes, blocking out anything but the sensation of his light touch, so delicate she barely felt the caress at first, but she was so sensitive it took nothing but the graze of a fingertip to make her throb.

Her breath rasped over the music. He stole one taste and she fisted her hand in his hair. Her stomach muscles knotted with excited need.

His caress deepened and she sobbed as glittering sensations poured through her. Her knees wanted to collapse, but she held very still as his lovemaking intensified and her arousal doubled upon itself until she was saying his name over and over, pushing her hips in an erotic rhythm and she was dying, *dying*, because it was so good.

Climax arrived as a wave of pleasure that had her tipping back her head to release her cry of joy toward the ceiling, body shuddering, hard hands on her hips the only way she remained standing.

"Your guards might have heard that," he said with smug lust, rising before her.

Her heart lurched.

His command of her and the moment stung. Not so much the guards hearing, although that was hideously embarrassing. No, it bothered her more that Kasim was significantly less affected by what had just happened than she was. She ought to be feeling like the selfish one, but it felt quite a bit like he had benefited from her giving up her self-control so thoroughly.

He guided her backward onto the sofa. She was so weak she fairly wilted onto it, body still shaking with aftershocks, but she was clearheaded enough to know she wanted him as carried away as she was.

He opened his belt, unzipped his fly and brought a condom from his pocket, all the while studying her like he had every right.

He covered himself and knelt between her knees, drawing her hips to the edge of the cushions and moving a pillow to the small of her back.

"That's very pretty," he said in a lust-filled voice.

The pillow arched her back so her breasts came up a few inches and he bent to suck her nipples again. It was proving to be her greatest weakness, making her close her thighs on his hips and urge him to soothe the ache he incited.

"Do you want me, Angelique?" He kissed her throat. "I want to hear it. Tell me."

"I do," she admitted on a helpless sob, not caring about propriety or modesty. But she did care that she not be alone in her abandonment to passion. She grasped the hot shape of him, feeling the muscle leap under her cautious caress, so hard and promising.

With a determination to make him as wild as she felt, she guided him to where she wanted him and caressed her folds with his tip.

He reared back, stole a look into her I-dare-you expression, and something untamed flashed in his gaze. He hooked his arms beneath her knees and nudged her for entry, pretty much daring her right back. *Take me, then,* he seemed to challenge.

She was very aroused and arched to accept him, but the press of him stretching her made her instinctively flinch. It had been a long time.

His grip on her legs prevented her from closing them, but he felt her reaction. He paused. "What's wrong?"

"Don't stop," she gasped, grabbing at his neck and pulling herself upward against him, angling her hips to take him in and releasing a stifled groan as he filled her.

He made a feral noise and shuddered.

"Gently," he ordered, moving in small, abbreviated strokes, testing her body's arousal and willingness to accept his intrusion.

She lolled back on the cushion, smiling at him in a way she had never imagined smiling at any man, inviting him to have his way with her. Thoroughly. Completely.

"Let them hear both of us this time," she taunted,

and ran her hands over her breasts, cupping them, letting her nipples poke from between her splayed fingers. "Unless you can't wait for me."

He muttered something that was probably an accusation of insolence, but he began moving with powerful strokes, deliberate and measured, watching her to ensure she liked it. She did, unable to help moaning and arching, hands stroking up his arms. She caught at his shoulders and pulled him down while bringing herself up, so they were chest to chest. She lifted her mouth to catch at his in soft, biting kisses.

Soon it became uninhibited and wild. Sweaty and earthy and abandoned. It was incredible. She would have laughed in triumph, but her breaths were nothing but jagged gasps and cries of pleasure. She received him with joy, basked in being his vessel, and told him how good he made her feel.

"Don't stop. Don't ever stop."

The tension built to impossible levels, both of them digging fingernails into the other as they mated, the enjoyment of the act no longer enough. They sought the culmination. It was coming. They were almost there. So close. Tense. Tight.

The world exploded and he covered her mouth with his own, so they were the only two who heard the sounds of ecstasy they made together.

CHAPTER FIVE

KASIM SHOULD HAVE been fast asleep. He was utterly relaxed. Sexually replete. He certainly didn't want to move. The bedsheets were smooth beneath his back, the warmth of Angelique draped over him the only blanket he needed. Her hair felt pleasantly extravagant, spilled across his chest and neck in cool ribbons.

She was falling asleep, twitching lightly as she drifted into slumber, growing heavier against him. Equally sated.

The things they had done to one another. He closed his eyes and a banquet of remembered sensation washed over him. Smooth, soft hands. A wet, lavish mouth. Legs like silk slithering against his own. Her ripples of climax squeezing him again and again.

Not that they'd been particularly adventurous. He generally left the level of exploit to his lover, never needing fancy positions or toys to enjoy himself so long as he had an eager partner. But the sofa hadn't been enough. They had come in here to the bedroom and consumed one another all over again.

It hadn't been mere enthusiasm between them. It had been immersion. For a woman who "didn't do this," Angelique was tremendously willing to throw herself into the fire of passion. He couldn't help but burn right alongside her.

Which was such a disturbing loss of self-governance, part of him was thinking he should rise and take her home right now.

His body reacted to the thought with an involuntary tightening of his arm around her. A fierce urge rocked through him to roll atop her and have her again.

One night was *not* enough.

Sleep, he ordered himself. *Sleep and think clearly in the morning.*

His eyes wouldn't stay closed, preferring to stare at the decorative ceiling tiles, textured with shadows in the mellow light slanting like sunset from the lounge.

He likened his sleeplessness to those few times in his life when a day had been so perfect, he couldn't make himself go to bed and end it. A day in the desert with his father as a child, when the king relaxed and they only concerned themselves with basic needs. Or his last day with his brother, *knowing* he would never see him again…

His heart gave a wrenching twist and he tensed, restraining himself from rolling into Angelique and seeking more than escape into physical pleasure. Comfort?

No. He refused to be that needy.

She drew a long inhale, disturbed by the tension that kept taking a grip on him. She repositioned herself, sighed and relaxed, but he could tell she was awake. He could feel her lashes blinking against his skin.

"I'm thirsty, but I don't want to move," she said in a husk of a voice.

He was starving, but only moved his hand to her head and caressed her scalp through the thick waves of her silky hair.

With a beleaguered sigh, she pulled away and climbed from the bed to go into the bathroom.

Kasim tucked his arm behind his head, listening to the tap run. When she came out of the bathroom in a robe, he rose onto his elbow.

"Come back to bed," he ordered, voice graveled by sexual excess.

"It's already been a very long dinner," she said wryly. "I don't want to give the press more fodder than they might already have." She walked out to the lounge.

Angelique was trembling on the inside, reacting to something so intense it had left her dismantled and exposed.

She gathered her few pieces of clothing and dressed, aware of Kasim coming into the lounge behind her, but she didn't turn to look at him. If she met his gaze, if he was naked, she feared she would find herself back in his bed in a matter of seconds.

With a practiced wriggle, she got the zip fastened up her back, then swept her loose hair back and behind her shoulders. The silk liner on the dress was cool and the beadwork made it feel heavy and stiff. Her sensitive, sensual soul was firmly tucked away behind walls and guards again.

Searching out her pocketbook, she glanced at her phone and saw her brother wanted her to text when she arrived home safely. She rolled her eyes and plucked her lipstick from the velvet interior of her purse. She had already tidied the rest of her face in the bathroom and was determined to look like she had *not* been rolling around with the prince all evening if she happened to be photographed leaving the hotel.

"You don't have to go."

"I should let you sleep," she said, sending him a sly look in the mirror near the door. "You've worked hard."

"That tongue," he said on a breath of laughter, stalking close to catch at her and turn her, drawing her in front of his naked frame. "If you hadn't used it to pleasure every inch of me, I would curse it completely."

Oh, he did not just say that. She blushed. Hard. And she would *not* look to see if he was laughing. Or hardening. She stared at the flex of tendons in his neck.

He chuckled and bent his head to nuzzle against her mouth with his own, murmuring, "I'm rather fond of it, now. Let me say hello again."

He meant "good night," didn't he?

Their lips parted and sealed in a mutual coming together, like polar opposites aligning and locking. His tongue found hers and caressed, making showers of pleasure tingle down her front. She hummed a pleasured noise and pressed into him, trying to assuage the instant rush of greedy desire.

She found him hard and famished. He clutched her with increasing passion, threatening Trella's beautiful beadwork.

She drew back as far as he would let her and had to stifle a pant of pure need. His eyes were like midnight, his desire for her undisguised, from the flush of excitement across his cheekbones to the thrust of flesh pressing into her abdomen.

"Come back to bed." Implacable determination was stamped into his face.

Her heart turned over with helpless yearning.

Defensive, flippant remarks like, *I had a nice time*, threatened to come to her lips, but she found herself speaking more earnestly. Almost begging for clemency. Her stupid eyes grew wet with the conflict inside her.

"I would prefer to keep tonight private, if at all possible." Her voice reflected the arousal he incited and the powerlessness she felt in the face of it. If he pressed, she would stay the night. "If I get caught doing the walk of shame tomorrow morning, it will cheapen something that was actually very nice." She couldn't bear that. She really couldn't.

His eyes narrowed in a brief flinch. His mouth tightened and she thought he was about to demand she stay anyway.

"I'm going to London tomorrow. Come with me."

She blinked, thrown. She had geared herself up for this to be one night. A rush of hope flooded her. *Yes. More.*

Just as quickly, she thought, *No. How?*

Her mind splintered at the complexity of it. Obligation to Trella rushed in to make anything but these few hours impossible.

"I thought... You seemed pretty clear about there being no future." She searched his gaze.

His expression grew shuttered. "One more night, that's all I'm talking about."

Ouch. Right. She smiled her regret, hoping he'd take it as regret at refusing, not the very real regret that this was such a dead-end road.

"The more we see each other, the more likely we are to become a sensation."

"Still trying to scare me off? It is unrealistic to think we won't be found out, that's true. So what? If that's the only obstacle, there is none."

"It's not," she murmured with genuine reluctance, and tried to step away. Maybe when she went to Berlin next week? She would have to think about it. She was never impetuous, least of all about men and allowing them to impact her life.

He locked his arms, not holding her more tightly, but

turning his muscles to steel so she was forced to stand quietly and look up at him. She did *not* hide her disapproval at being manhandled.

"What then?" he queried.

"Trella is coming to Paris."

"So?"

"We have to finish your sister's trousseau."

"Hasna will not be wearing everything you're giving her on her first day of marriage. I will personally take responsibility for anything that arrives late."

"That's not the point." She tried again to pivot away from him.

He kept her in place, not allowing her to screen her emotions or remove herself from his thought-scattering touch. *Infuriating.*

"I never leave Trella alone when she's here." She'd never even considered it because she'd never been tempted. She set her hands on his wrists where he gripped her hips, trying to extricate herself from the lure of him. "Most especially not overnight."

"How old are you?"

"Twenty-four. And don't pass judgment." She could see opinions forming behind his eyes and it was true that they all babied Trella, but there were *reasons.*

Trella was traveling on her own tomorrow, though. Did that mean she was ready for other acts of independence?

Angelique found herself standing acquiescent in Kasim's embrace, considering her own arguments to her brothers about allowing Trella room to find her own confidence.

What if she had a rebound crash as a result, though? She was trying to justify deserting her sister. What was wrong with her?

Berlin, she thought again, because it was further into the future and gave her time to think. This man moved way too fast for her.

"Is security the issue? Your detail can travel with us," he said.

"No. I mean, yes, they would have to. And Henri keeps a flat in London that is completely secure. No, it's Trella. I could ask her…"

"I do not ask permission from strangers to go away with my lover."

"That's not— You don't understand." *Lover.* Her heart pounded with excitement at the sound of that.

"Enlighten me."

"No," she said bluntly. She never talked about Trella's experience. It was hers and nearly killed Angelique every time she revisited it. Her nostrils stung with unshed tears just thinking about it.

His fingertips dug in just a little against the soft flesh of her hips, insisting on possessing her full attention.

"Am I sleeping with you or your sister, Angelique?"

"That's the problem, Kasim. That is exactly the problem," she said as her eyes filled.

Kasim had begun to think she was playing coy, attempting a manipulation as some women were inclined, but the anguish in her beautiful features was real. It caused such a twist of protectiveness in him, he instinctively tightened his arms to draw her nearer.

The old habit of standing between Jamal and the constant threat of harm rose in him, mentally pushing him between Angelique and her sister, making him even more determined to separate her from something that was obviously harming her in some way.

She resisted his attempt to enfold her, bottom lip caught in her teeth, brow pulled into a wrinkle of angst.

With a flex of agitation at the stiffness of her, he pulled away and sought out his pants from the floor where he'd shed them.

"Explain," he commanded as he stepped into them and zipped. He reached for his shirt, slipping it on but leaving it unbuttoned.

"It's hard," she said in a small voice, one hand lifting helplessly. "It doesn't even make sense, really. But it's how I feel." She sighed heavily. "And I am the sensitive one, ruled by my emotions."

She sounded so forlorn.

He folded his arms, trying not to let that niggle at him. He had learned to shield himself against expressions of deep emotion. Too many times in his childhood he'd been bombarded by the pain of others—his mother and Fatina, the king's warring wives, trying to draw him to their side. Jamal's inner torture then Hasna's unrelenting grief…

There was no way to fix the emotional pain of others. He could only protect himself from becoming wound up in it.

Seeing Angelique had demons warned him to cut short whatever this was, but he found himself rooted, willing her to speak. He wanted to understand why she was resisting him. He wanted to help her.

"It was supposed to be me," she said, gaze naked and filled with guilty torment. "The kidnapping. I was the quiet one. The shy one. The one who was bad at math and needed a tutor. It was end of semester and our chauffeur was coming. Trella was already outside. She was the extrovert who wanted to say goodbye to everyone. My tutor called out to her. He thought she was me.

She went over to tell him I would be out soon and he grabbed her." She snapped her fingers. "Just like that. Ramon came out in time to see it happen and chased the van as far as he could, but they'd plotted their getaway very well…"

Her lips were white. Her hand shook as she tucked her hair behind her ear.

"Was she…?" He didn't want to finish the question. What kind of person assaulted a nine-year-old child?

"What happened in those five days is Trella's to tell or not," Angelique said in a voice that quavered. She knew, though. The answer was in her eyes. *Hell.* Whatever it was, it had been hell.

Kasim moved to take her cold hands in his, trying to rub warmth into them.

"You're suffering survivor's guilt," he said quietly. "I understand that." He did. Jamal should be living the life Kasim enjoyed. They were both sons of the king. There was no difference between them except those small characteristics that made every person unique unto themselves.

"The guilt is only part of it. We were already legendary, not that we ever wanted that sort of notoriety, but that's why we were targeted. The Sauveterre Twins, one of Europe's treasures, right? Of course payment would be made for Trella's return. Of course the press went mad at the sensationalism of it."

She cleared her throat, obviously struggling.

"My father had to use that circus to our advantage. I looked just like Trella so they used me as Trella's face, to plea for her return. Any tiny thing could have been the key to getting her back. It was horrible exploitation. He hated himself for doing it to me, but when you're desperate…"

Her eyes filled and she pulled her hand out of his to press the knot of her fist between her breasts.

"All the while… The connection between twins is a real thing, Kasim. It is for Trella and me. I knew she was terrified and suffering. It was unbearable. And then she came back to us so broken and I felt that, too." Her lips quivered.

He had to enfold her in his arms. Had to.

She shook like a tiny animal that had barely escaped certain death.

"She's safe now, hmm?" he coaxed gently into her hair. "Come back, Angelique. That was a long time ago and she's safe. You're both safe now."

She nodded and sniffed once, but he could feel the shudders of dark memory running through her. Her arms went around his waist, beneath his open shirt. The beadwork on her dress abraded his bare skin. He stroked her hair, imparting as much comfort as he could, rubbing his chin against her temple.

"You're afraid to leave her alone, in case something happens again," he surmised.

"I'm afraid all the time of everything." Her cheek was damp where she pressed it to his chest. "That's who I am, Kasim. I'm the worrier. I'm the introvert. But I had to become the strong one. The only way I've ever been able to do that— God, the only way I could find the courage to stand in front of cameras and beg for her return was to pretend I was her. I had to become her in some ways. How could I ever go back to being quiet, shy Angelique who leaned on her sister for confidence? My support was shattered. She needed *me* to be that person."

She wiped at her cheek and settled against him again.

"We should be two carefree young women, but she

was cheated. I know she would have risen to the challenge if it had been me so I have to do that for her. Everything I do is for both of us. Sometimes I feel like I am her and I don't know how to be just me."

Her odd comment at dinner about being each other, which he had thought was a bit of twin peculiarity, now made more sense. So did the one about her not letting herself "be."

"Who were you tonight?" he asked, cupping the side of her neck, invaded by a prickling tension as he urged her to look up at him.

She drew back, but her gaze stayed on her own fingertips as she smoothed the hairs down his breastbone in a petting caress that made shivers of delight travel up his spine.

"I stole tonight for myself."

"Good. That is the correct answer."

She tsked and gave him a little shove. He only settled her closer, pleased when she relaxed and rested her head against his shoulder again, arms looped around his waist.

"But I can't be selfish and take what I want. I can't do that to Trella. Do you understand?"

"You know you cannot live someone else's life for them, don't you?" How many times had he tried to solve Jamal's "problem" to no avail? "You cannot shelter someone forever. It's not fair to either of you. We are each responsible for our own lives."

"I know," she murmured. "Separating my life from my sister's has to happen. We both know that. But I can't force that on her and I certainly won't let you force it. And the truth is…" She tilted back her head to look up at him with a solemn expression. "I am not impulsive. I am a thinker. If you want Angelique to go anywhere with you, you have to give *Angelique* time to put it all together in her pretty little head."

He pondered that, distantly aware he didn't have much time. His father was already talking about finding him a bride as soon as Hasna's wedding was out of the way.

"How much time do you need? I was going to leave first thing in the morning and it's already…" He looked around and swore lightly. "There are no such things as clocks anymore."

Releasing her, he found his cell phone and clicked to see it was nearing midnight. He dropped the phone into his pocket, then left his hand there with it. He raised the other to pinch his bottom lip.

"I have meetings in the morning. Come later in the day. I'll make the arrangements."

"I can make my own arrangements," she informed him, but with a rueful purse of her lips. "Which I realize you just heard as agreement." She sighed and touched her brow. "I could call my mother, see if she feels like spending the night in Paris with Trella. Does anyone ever say no to you, Kasim?"

"They realize very quickly that it is a waste of both our time. You, apparently, are a slow learner."

"Don't," she said with a little flinch. "It's still a sore point for me. I can cut out a perfect square meter of fabric by sight, but ask me to add one half to three quarters and I just embarrass myself. Now I'm going to put on fresh lipstick." Her hand shook as she picked up the little golden tube and pointed it at him. "Keep your lips to yourself."

"Come here first," he commanded, compelled to reinforce the connection between them.

She paused in winding up the stick of color, sent

him a pert look. "Saying 'no' would just be a waste of a layer of lipstick, wouldn't it?"

"Look at you. You're actually very quick to learn."

She rolled her eyes, but she came across to kiss him.

CHAPTER SIX

IF I NEED YOU, I'll call.

Trella's words dogged Angelique as she stole off to London. They weren't telling any of the family that Angelique was leaving Trella for a night on her own in Paris. Better to let it be a fait accompli, they decided, given how reluctant their brothers had been to let Trella make the short flight alone.

Trella had passed her own test "with flying colors," she had excitedly said about her solitary flight, quite triumphant in her achievement.

Angelique had been so proud, she'd had a little cry about it, which had made Trella laugh and hug her and call her their sensitive little Gili.

Nevertheless, Angelique felt guilty for leaving. Trella was very safe. Situated on the top floor of the design house, the Paris flat was ultra-secure. Seamstresses and other staff came and went from the lower floors, working into the night if the mood took, but the flat had its own entrance, a panic room and a private passage to the office.

Trella had been very heartfelt in her plea for Angelique to do something for herself for a change.

I've held you back too long, Trella had insisted, then added with a sly look, *Besides, I'm curious about Henri and Cinnia. See what you can find out.*

Angelique had laughed at that, but if Trella had a setback, she would never forgive herself.

Deep down, however, she was anxious to see Kasim again. It was a foreign state of mind for her. After Trella's experience, she'd spent her adolescence wary of boys and sex. When she finally started to date, she had been hard-pressed to find men who measured up to the standards her father and brothers had set. When her suitors had fallen off because her life was too restrictive, or proved to be social climbers or other opportunists, she'd been annoyed and disappointed, but never truly hurt.

She had never been taken with any man. None had engaged her feelings very deeply and she had never, ever, allowed a man to come between her and her family.

In some ways, she was terrified of the influence Kasim was having on her. He fascinated her and thus had power over her. He was confident and secure in himself, almost brutally honest, but that lack of subterfuge was as seductive as the rest of him.

And oh, did he seduce! From a physical standpoint, she was completely infatuated. Her blood raced as she silently willed the driver into London after the family jet landed at the private airfield.

She hadn't given Trella many details about her evening with Kasim, but her sister had said with a sensual lift of her own hair, *I know you slept with him. Don't deny it. I'm kind of jealous, actually. In a good way. It makes me realize what I'm missing.*

That had made Angelique very self-conscious, but she knew Trella was interpreting her body language. They had the same expressions and mannerisms so even though Angelique could disguise her thoughts and feelings from many, her sister would read the indolent stretch or the warmed cheek and soft gaze of pleasant memory without effort.

Trella didn't tease her for it, and when Angelique studied Trella, she saw nothing but determination in her sister at being left alone this evening.

Kasim had been right about Angelique suffering survivor's guilt. She wondered if it was the reason she had given up so easily on her previous relationships. Being happy when her sister had been struggling had always felt incredibly disloyal.

She still felt disloyal, haring off to London to be with a man, but it was only one night, she told herself. Kasim hadn't promised anything else and neither had she for that matter, even though she felt a yearning for more.

Not that she'd defined exactly what "more" would be. The artist in her appreciated that whatever they had was too new and special for close examination. Deconstruction could kill it. Sometimes you had to go with instinct, then determine after the fact what you had.

Was this instinct? Or greed and selfishness? Or old-fashioned blindness to obvious facts?

Exactly the type of scrutiny she had to avoid, she thought with a stifled sigh.

Whatever it was, it drew her inexorably. Her pulse was racing over a single text from Kasim, promising to meet her at her brother's flat within the hour.

It was actually the family flat. Knowing Henri was in New York, Angelique assumed Cinnia was staying in her own flat, but texted her as a courtesy, mentioning that she was in town and asking if Cinnia wanted to get together for a meal.

Cinnia's reply came through as Angelique was let-

ting herself in. It was a simple regret that she was staying with her mother and was sorry she had missed the
chance to visit.

Angelique put her bag in the room she and Trella
used, checked that there was a decent bottle of wine in
the fridge and moved restlessly into the lounge, wondering if she and Kasim were going out for dinner and
if so, where? What should she wear?

Paparazzi. Ugh, she thought with another sigh, but
for once she wasn't filled with as much dread as usual.
She would have hated to have her night with Kasim reduced by the online trolls to a one-night stand, sullied
and mocked, even though she'd gone to his room last
night convinced it would be only that.

Having this affair extend into a second night made it
feel— Well, it still felt so rare and precious she wanted
to guard it jealously, but she was so thrilled to see him
again, she was willing to pay the price.

"Oh, no," she murmured, jerked from introspection
as she caught sight of the coffee table.

A courier envelope had been torn open and the contents spilled out. It was at least a hundred thousand
euros in jewelry, probably more. It looked like the contents of Ali Baba's cave, glittering and sparkling inno-
cently against the glass tabletop.

Angelique sat down hard on the sofa, chest tight. She
thought about texting Trella, but Henri was the most
private of all of them. He would kill her if he knew *she*
had seen this. She couldn't share it like tawdry gossip,
not even with Trella.

But what had gone wrong?

Henri was adamant in his decision never to marry, but
he and Cinnia had seemed so good together. Angelique
would have bet real money that Cinnia genuinely loved

him. How had those tender feelings become something as harsh as throwing his gifts back in his face?

It was a cool, disturbing reminder that relationships fell into one of two categories: those with a future and those that ended. Her heart chilled, starkly confronted with the kind she had with Kasim.

There wouldn't be a moment of callous rejection between them, though. Not like this. She and Kasim were never going to spend two years together the way Henri had with Cinnia.

Upset for Henri and Cinnia—and disturbed on her own behalf—she pushed the jewelry into the envelope, but the artist in her was drawn to examine the tennis bracelet. She'd never taken a proper look at it. It was a string of alternating pink and white diamonds, one Cinnia had always seemed to be wearing. Angelique was really shocked she'd given it up, especially now that she saw how exquisite it really was. The craftsmanship in the setting was extraordinary. She searched it for an insignia that might tell her where it had come from.

When the door opened behind her, she stood with surprise, expecting Maurice, but it was Kasim. She had told Maurice to expect him, but had thought she'd have to ring him through the main doors downstairs before he would appear up here.

"How did you get in the building?" she asked as she moved to meet him, flushing uncontrollably with instant pleasure.

His mouth tilted with a hint of smugness, as if he read her infatuation and knew how slowly the minutes had passed for her before seeing him again. It was disconcerting, making her feel defenseless and obvious, but she still found herself crossing toward him, tugged by an invisible lasso around her middle.

He waited for the door to shut before he hooked his arm around her and kissed her.

It was proprietary and given how fleeting this affair was likely to be, she should be keeping better control over herself, but her heart soared. She quickly melted into him, instantly transported to the languorous memories of last night and anticipation for more of the same incredible pleasure he'd delivered.

"You missed me," he said when he drew back.

"You didn't miss me?" She tried to sound blasé, tried to pull away, but she was hyperaware of how needy that sounded. How completely easy she was being.

His hand slid to her tailbone and pressed her hips into his enough that she felt how he was reacting to her. "I've been thinking about you," he allowed.

Fluttery joy invaded her abdomen and she tried not to reveal how quickly and thoroughly he'd bowled her over.

"Good to know," she said lightly. "But I am genuinely curious how you got into the building. It's supposed to be locked down for residents only."

"It is. I was given the codes when I bought my flat this morning. Shall we go look at it?" He finally released her and stepped toward the door with a low wave for her to accompany him.

"You—you bought a unit in this building *this morning*?" She had grown up with wealth, but they only owned a flat here because her father had bought it during the design stage, just before his death. The address was obscenely exclusive with a wait list a mile long of international dignitaries and techno-billionaires trying to get in.

Perhaps she had underestimated *how* wealthy and

powerful Kasim was. The cost to jump queue must have been exorbitant.

"It's a good investment. My mother likes London," he said with a shrug. "She'll use it if I don't. Mostly I thought you'd appreciate the privacy. By some miracle, there is nothing online about us. I thought we'd celebrate our lack of infamy by staying in and extending our lucky streak. I've ordered dinner to be delivered in a couple of hours."

"We could have stayed here!" she pointed out.

He offered a pained frown. "I do not steal into a girl's bedroom at her parents' home."

No, he dropped a few million pounds on a suite he was only using for one night. *For her.*

She urged herself not to let that mean too much.

"Shall I change?" She was still wearing her travel clothes, a dark blue jersey skirt with a pale yellow top, both her own design. They were quietly feminine, breezy yet classic and a tiny bit waifish.

"You look beautiful." He skimmed his gaze down and back. "And whatever you wear is only for the elevator."

"You're not even going to pretend you're inviting me to look at etchings?" She planted her hands on her hips, only realizing as she did that she was still holding Cinnia's bracelet. Shoot. She was instantly self-conscious on her brother's behalf. "Um. I just have to put this down and grab my phone."

"What is it?" Kasim asked, catching at her wrist as the snaking sparkle caught his attention.

She opened her hand. "Something Henri bought for Cinnia," she prevaricated.

Her brother's long-term relationship was well documented in the press, but she wasn't going to be the one to start the rumors about its demise.

"I want to ask him where he got it because the work is outstanding. Look at the detail here. You can tell each of these claws has been crimped individually to create this effect all the way along. I'm in awe at how painstaking that would be. Have you ever seen anything like it?"

Kasim's nostrils flared as he picked up the bracelet and gave it a thorough study, his expression pulling into a tension that bordered on agony. As if suddenly realizing how hard he was staring, and that she was watching him, he quickly straightened his features and handed her the bracelet.

"No," he answered belatedly and rather abruptly. "Let's go."

Her heart did a little thump. The mood had definitely shifted. "What's wrong?"

"Nothing."

She was hurt that he would lie so blatantly to her, but moved across to tuck the bracelet into the envelope and picked up her phone.

The silence in the elevator was not precisely thick, but it was significant.

Kasim's cheeks were hollow, his mouth flat.

Maurice was with them, so Angelique kept her own counsel. Her guard went through Kasim's new flat ahead of them, even though Kasim's team had been here all day, ensuring it was not only clean and secure, but furnished and well stocked.

The layout was similar to her family's suite with a lounge opening onto a balcony overlooking the Thames. She imagined the door next to the wet bar led to the kitchen, as it did in their own. Down the hall would be the bedrooms and baths.

This one smelled faintly of paint and was filled with contemporary furniture and a handful of decent art pieces. His decorator was competent, if unimaginative, having fallen back on the latest issue of *Colors of the Year* for lack of inspiration.

The moment Maurice left them alone, Kasim drew her into his arms again and kissed her quite passionately. Almost aggressively, questing for a response. It was as if he was trying to propel them into the mindless state they'd experienced last night in Paris.

It was breathlessly exciting, yet made her feel… She wasn't sure and, as her blood began to heat, started not to care.

"Do I not even get a chance to explore the place myself?" she gasped when his mouth traveled to the side of her neck. Arousal suffused her, but she had the sense she was being used as much as desired. It scraped her insides raw.

"If you like," he said, straightening and not looking pleased.

"Have you even seen it?" she asked, trying to recover and stung by the distance she sensed between them.

"I'm more interested in this." His lashes cut downward as he slid his gaze to her toes and came back to her lips.

His ravenous gaze made her skin tighten, but her heart squeezed at the same time. She *knew* he was sublimating something.

"Kasim." She cupped his jaw. "What has upset you?"

"I'm not upset." He pulled away from her touch and moved to the bar. "Children get upset. Do you want wine?"

He was speaking shortly. Irritably. Like he was upset, she thought drily.

"Something about the bracelet bothered you. Did you recognize it?" She was intuitive that way. She just was.

"You can tell me what it was, or I can make up stories of my own to explain your reaction."

"I've never seen it," he said flatly, setting out two wineglasses. "But the workmanship reminded me of Jamal's. He designed jewelry."

He wound the screw into the cork with a little squeaking noise and pulled it out with a pop, movements jerky, facial muscles still tense.

"My father hated it. He took it as a reflection against his own masculinity. An insult. He was ashamed to have a son who was…artistic," he pronounced with disdain. "My mother used that to her advantage."

"What do you mean?"

He poured, steadying the bottoms of each glass with two fingers as he did.

"Jamal is—was Fatina's son. My father's second wife. My mother…"

He set aside the bottle. For a moment he was a man on the verge of exploding, wrapped tightly, but packed to the eyebrows with dynamite, fuse burning in his eyes.

"Children should not be used as weapons, but my mother loved to find fault with him. To his face, to my father, in public. However she could humiliate him and Fatina, she did it. In sly ways, though. Small little stabs. Death by a thousand cuts," he said grimly.

"That's horrible."

"It was. And my father was determined to turn him into something he could be proud of. That was his way of countering my mother's attacks, by telling Jamal he was to blame for her criticisms. If he only changed, we would all have peace. I'm furious every time I'm reminded of how it was for him."

"You couldn't make your father see reason?"

He snorted. "This?" He lifted his glass and touched

it to the rim of hers. "I don't care one way or another for alcohol, but it is completely outlawed in Zhamair. It's not a religious restriction. We have as many citizens who are Christian or Jewish as we do Muslims in our country, but my father's word is rule. My father is a dictator in the way that political scientists define one."

"But you do what you want when you're away," she noted with a glance at his Western clothes. "Couldn't your brother have done that? I'm sorry, I know it's very easy to say that he should leave his country and turn his back on his father. It's not something anyone would do without deep struggle, but…"

"No," Kasim agreed in a hard, grim voice. "It's not. Especially since it meant leaving his mother and the rest of his siblings. Fatina has four younger children, as well. And he felt my father's rejection very deeply. He wanted desperately to earn his respect. It was an impossible situation for him."

"That's so awful." Her heart ached for not just his brother, but for Kasim. No wonder he wanted to take the reins from a man who possessed no hint of compassion or empathy. No wonder he had fought so hard for Hasna to have a love marriage.

"How did he die?" she asked softly, then clutched where the pang in her chest had intensified. She could see the anguish still fresh in Kasim's face. "It wasn't suicide, was it?"

Kasim didn't speak, only stared into his wine for a long moment. His fingernails were so white where he clutched the stem of his glass, she though he would snap the crystal. His gaze came up and she thought he looked about to say something.

In the next second, he shut down, mouth flattening into a sealed line before he finally said in a neutral, almost practiced, voice, "It was a car crash. We were in Morocco on business. He was out on his own along a stretch of road near the ocean. He wasn't reckless by nature, but he was under a lot of pressure from my father to give up the jewelry design, work with me full-time and marry suitably."

His expression was filled with perturbed memories.

"The car went through the guardrail into the rocks below. Calling my father with the news was hard, but facing Fatina and Hasna, and my younger brothers and sisters…"

The torment in his expression was too much to bear. So much guilt, but how could he have prevented it? It was just a terrible accident. He shouldn't blame himself.

She set aside her glass and came around the bar to slide her arms around his waist. "I'm sorry."

"Why? You had nothing to do with it." He continued to hold his glass, his other arm hanging at his side, stiff and unresponsive to her embrace. He looked down his nose at her.

"I shouldn't have forced you to revisit his loss."

She felt the flinch go through him. He sipped, stony as a column of marble that didn't give under the lean of her weight, only supported her with cold, indifferent strength. "The bracelet did that."

"And you wanted me to help you think of nicer things." She traced her fingertips up the line of his spine through the back of his shirt, trying to reach him through physical contact since he seemed to have shut her out emotionally. "Now I will. If you like."

"What about your great explore?" He didn't bend at all.

"I've seen a flat just like this one. But this…" She brought her hands around to climb his chest and brush his suit jacket open, nudging it to fall back off his shoulders. "This territory is still new to me."

She was trying to be bold, to find the affinity they had shared in Paris, but was highly unsure when he failed to respond. Self-doubt, her great nemesis, twisted through her.

"I plan to be very thorough in my mapping of it," she said, voice wavering as she became convinced he was about to reject her.

"You're liable to see nothing but this ceiling for the next hour," he warned, setting aside his glass and clasping her hips in heavy hands.

"Maybe that's all *you'll* see," she said with a tremble of relief. "Did you think of that?"

Kasim had almost told her the truth about Jamal. It was a stunning break in his normal vigilance against any woman's intrusion into his inner world.

Idly caressing from the back of her thigh over the curve of her buttock to the hollow in the small of her back, he wondered how this smooth golden skin had come to get so far under his own in such a short amount of time.

He didn't regard women as a Western indulgence he allowed himself when he traveled, but he did treat his sexual relationships much as he did his business ones. Some were brief transactions, some longer term, but they were exchanges and trades, always agreements with clear parameters. Paramours didn't cause him to rearrange his life and they rarely stimulated more than his libido.

This one, however... He had made a ridiculously large transfer this morning so he could protect their privacy, mindful of her request last night to keep the world from cheapening their association.

Why? What did he care if their association was known or in what context? He would eagerly show her off. The idea of staking a public claim held a great deal of pleasure for him, in fact.

He very carefully blocked the vision of any other man thumbing into the small dimples at the top of each of her firm, round cheeks, then he lightly traced the line that separated them, fingertips claiming Angelique's backside along with the rest of her, sweeping the back of her thigh and taking possession of her calf.

He had grown up watching his father deal with the fallout of indulging unfettered lust. Every person was susceptible to being attracted to the wrong person— or rather, an inconvenient person in relation to the life they led. Giving in to that desire was the root of whatever problems arose.

Kasim had always regarded himself as superior to his father and brother. *He* was capable of rising above the temptations that foretold complications.

Was he kidding himself, believing this thing with Angelique was a trouble-free dalliance that could end tomorrow morning with a light kiss and a "pleasant knowing you"?

An uncomfortable bolt of rejection shot through him, not just resisting the idea of walking away, but outright refusing to countenance it. His reaction was so visceral, his hand closed in a small squeeze where it rested above the back of her knee. He was literally holding on to her and he'd only *thought* about the inevitable parting that awaited them.

It was a sobering confrontation with his inner animal, the one he had always been so sure he governed without effort.

"I'm awake," she murmured on a contented sigh,

as if she took his grip to be a test of her level of consciousness.

She turned her head so she could blink dreamy eyes at him while keeping her face mostly buried in her folded arms and the fall of her magnificent hair. "Just thinking. Do you want to meet me in Berlin next weekend? I have a thing."

He had places to be, people to rise above.

"I thought we were staying out of the spotlight."

Her sleepy smile slowly warmed to something vulnerable yet elated. It made his heart swerve and swell.

"I was really asking if you wanted to see me again after tonight." The tone in her voice caused a pleasant-painful vibration through him.

He looked at where his hand was still firm on the back of her thigh. "I fear for our lives at the rate we're going, but I was going to ask you to stay the weekend. I have to escort my mother and sister back to Zhamair on Sunday, but I will arrange to take them back late." He would also cancel his lunch arrangements for tomorrow with his foreign secretary and the British counterpart.

"I wasn't planning to spend the weekend," she said, last night's troubled light coming into her eye. Her sister again.

"No?" He tensed and felt her hamstring flex against his light grip.

Guilt and longing fought for dominance in her gaze. She released a soft moan of struggle and gave a taut stretch beneath his touch.

"I will if I can arrange it." Her tone echoed with something like defeat.

He began to pet her again, blood tingling as he fondled her with more purpose. He wasn't used to a woman resisting him. It made him restless for her capitulation.

Not something forced. No, he needed her to give herself up to him.

Rolling her over, he began to kiss her, running his mouth to all the places that made her arch and moan under him, impressing on her the benefit of belonging to him. As he felt the tension in her, the clasp of nearing climax, he kissed his way back up the center of her torso.

"Tell me what you want."

"You know," she sobbed, moving against his hand, but he followed her undulations, keeping his penetration shallow and light.

"You want this?" he very slowly and gently deepened his caress, deliberately holding her on the plane of acute pleasure she occupied, not letting her tumble into orgasm. "Or this?"

He rolled atop her and loved the saw of her breath as she gasped in a sensual agony. Holding himself in a tight fist, fighting back from his own approaching peak, he rubbed his aching tip against her slick folds, nudging at her with promise.

She danced and angled her hips, trying to capture him.

He shook with want, barely able to see straight, but made himself hold off and only kiss her. "What will you do for me?"

"Anything," she gasped, but opened her eyes. They were shiny with helpless torture, a hint of resentment even. She knew what he was demanding. *Her.*

He cupped her head and slowly, slowly sank into her. Their breaths mingled as their bodies joined, both of them parting their lips to release jagged noises of intense pleasure.

How could she resent this? How?

He made love to her then, sending her over the edge, then keeping her aroused so they were damned near clawing each other when the next crest approached. He didn't think he could wait for her, but he wanted her with him. Demanded it with the hard thrust of his hips against her. *Needed it.*

She locked herself around him and released a keening noise, shuddering beneath him. The greedy clasp of her sheath triggered his own climax and he shouted in triumph as he joined her in the paroxysm.

Angelique was a little stunned by what she'd just experienced. Not just the ferocity of Kasim's lovemaking. She'd been so aroused, she had craved that intensity, but there'd been a loss of self in that joining. He had been the only thing important to her. It left her scrambling to recover her sense of autonomy, while he made it impossible by rolling back into her and running proprietary hands over her still-tingling skin.

The condom was gone along with his urgency. Now he was the tender man whose touch was soothing and reassuring. He almost lulled her back into thinking everything about him was safe, but it wasn't. He imperiled the very heart of her.

She put up an instinctive hand against his chest, resisting his effort to pull her into a sprawl across his sweat-damp body.

"What's wrong?" He picked up her hand and lightly bit her fingertip, then kissed the same spot. "I can't make promises about Berlin, but I will try. Good enough?"

He sounded languid and satisfied while she was completely dismantled.

"Is it because we might be found out?" She had been

trying to think how they could continue on the sly, but couldn't see a way, not unless he wanted to go broke buying private flats. He hadn't seemed particularly worried about exposure anyway. "Would it be complicated for you with Hasna if something wound up in the press?"

He snorted. "I don't consult *my* sister on how I conduct my private life."

There. *That* was the issue. He resented her sister. She stiffened and tried to pull away.

"That was a cheap shot," he allowed, arms clamping like a straitjacket around her. "I take it back."

"No!" She turned her face away. "You don't get to kiss me into forgetting you said it."

He sighed against her cheek.

"I'm spoiled," he stated without compunction. "Never second fiddle to anyone except my father and that is a finite situation, not that I wish his life away. I only mean that I am his heir and aside from him, I am autonomous."

"Yet I'm supposed to be content as a second fiddle in your life."

A long pause that was so loaded, she had to glance warily at him, fearful she'd truly angered him.

Maybe she hadn't angered him, but she'd scored a point. She could see echoes of his mood earlier when he'd talked about his mother's brutal treatment of his father's second wife and his half brother.

"I have meetings all next week," he said in a cool tone. "Roundtable discussions with a dozen of our region's most powerful leaders. You must have an idea of our political and economic landscape? The stakes are always high. I go so my father won't or he'll send us back to the Stone Age. The conference could easily go into next weekend. That is the only reason I am avoiding saying yes to Berlin."

"Fine." Now she felt like she'd pressured a concession of sorts from him, but it was a hollow victory. "It was just a thought."

"What are you doing there?" His tone wasn't patronizing, but she read his question as an attempt to mollify her and move past their conflict.

"A fashion awards night." She glossed over it. "There's a white tie and champagne thing after. I'm presenting so I can't skip it. You'd probably find it boring anyway."

"Do you do a lot of these things? Who do you usually go with?"

She would not kid herself that he sounded jealous.

"Colleagues. Sometimes one of my brothers. Honestly, it's fine. I'm supposed to be at a thing tonight and—" She'd forgotten to cancel, she realized. She had decided not to go once she realized Trella would be in town, but had paid the plate fee because it was a charity she liked to support. It wasn't a big deal that she was a no-show. She shouldn't be experiencing this stab of guilt.

All part of Kasim's magnifying effect on her emotions, she supposed. She frowned, aware of a cloud of traitorousness blanketing her too, along with a niggling desire to rebel. She put it all down to letting him extract that surrender to his seduction at the expense of thinking of—

She scrambled out of his arms to sit up. *Trella*.

"What—?" Kasim made a noise.

She kicked away the covers as she scooted off the bed. "I have to check in with Trella."

"Why?"

"I just do," she muttered and quickly shrugged into his robe, tying it tight then leaving to scour the lounge for her cell phone.

Angelique had put down the agitation in her belly to the sound of an invisible clock ticking down on her time with Kasim and all the things that she was doing that were out of character: engaging in an affair, leaving her sister, shunning work responsibilities.

But there was that other plane of awareness that her sister occupied in her unconscious…

Kasim came into the lounge, pants pulled on, but wearing nothing else, blanking her mind. Lord, he was beautiful, moving with economy, sculpted muscles rippling under smooth, swarthy skin. For a moment she forgot to breathe, she was so captivated.

He prowled to where the food had been received and abandoned on the dining table an hour ago. They had been too busy with each other when it arrived to do more than set it aside and get back to bed.

He opened the wicker basket and said, "We should eat before this is stone cold."

When he glanced at her, he caught her ogling. A light smirk touched his gorgeous mouth. He hooked his thumbs in his waistband, so sexy her mouth watered.

"Unless you're hungry for something else?"

She swallowed and ignored the fact her blood turned to lava. It was better that he wouldn't be in Berlin. He had way too much power over her as it was.

"I could eat." She hid her reaction by gathering their still-full wineglasses and bringing them across to the table under his watchful eye.

"Your sister?" he prompted.

"Fine." She bit her lip, flashing him an uncertain look. "She told me not to hurry back."

Take advantage of flying under the radar as long as you can, Trella had texted, but Angelique was still aware of her sister in that peripheral way. Trella wasn't frightened precisely, but she was disturbed.

They had used their authentication codes, though. She knew it was definitely Trella telling her to stay in London, coming across like an adolescent pushing for independence, insisting she was *completely fine*.

Angelique hadn't tried a video call, too embarrassed at how much she would betray, especially wearing Kasim's robe.

"So you'll stay the weekend." Kasim looped his arm around her.

"Do I have a choice?" she challenged tartly.

He stroked the back of his bent finger along her jaw, perhaps looking apologetic, but all he said was "Not if I have anything to do with it, no."

Then he kissed her until she was leaning into him, utterly spellbound.

CHAPTER SEVEN

Aside from the odd time when she had become tipsy from having too little to eat before having a glass of wine, Angelique had never been drunk or stoned. Kasim, however, provoked a feeling in her that she imagined one felt when ingesting party pills.

She walked around in a fog of euphoria after London, mood swinging wildly. One minute she was lost in recalling how they had essentially spent two solid days in bed, rising only to eat and make love elsewhere in the flat: the sofa, the kitchen chair, the shower. It made her too blissed out to care about the lost shipment of linen or the hundreds of euros in hand-made bobbin lace that wound up attached to the wrong gown.

The next minute she plummeted into a withdrawal depression, certain she'd never hear from him again. With his hand buried in her hair, he had kissed her deeply late Sunday afternoon, both of them aware cars and planes were waiting for them. He had finally released her, saying, "You won't hear from me. I'll be tied up in meetings. I'll try to meet you in Berlin. If I can't, we'll figure out something for the following week."

Would they, though? She wished they'd made a clean break of it. She could have handled that. This veering between hope and despair was too much!

If Trella noticed Angelique's distraction, she didn't say anything. She was immersed in finishing Hasna's wardrobe, almost obsessing over each piece, working late and rising early to ensure everything was perfect. She seemed really wound up about it when she was usually the coolheaded one about deadlines and never lacked confidence that their work would be received with great enthusiasm.

Angelique had a fleeting thought that her sister was burying herself in work to avoid her, but they *were* behind, thanks to Angelique staying in London an extra day. It was probably her own distraction making it seem like her sister was off. She was grateful to Trella for picking up the slack and tried to set her own nose to the grindstone so they could ship everything as planned.

Then, even though time passed at a glacial pace, she suddenly found herself rattling around her hotel room in Berlin, phone in hand as she compulsively checked her messages for word from Kasim, behaving exactly like an addict needing a fix. She had sent him her agenda yesterday, mildly panicked at the lack of word from him. She absolutely refused to let herself text again.

Tonight's event was taking place here in this brand-new hotel. Her suite was airy and ultra-contemporary, run by a firm out of Dubai that understood the meaning of luxury. She promised herself a soak in the private whirlpool tub when she returned later. It was already filled and warmed. Tiny whorls of steam wisped from the edge of its rollback cover and candles were at hand, awaiting a match.

She would need to drown some sorrows since it looked like Kasim wouldn't turn up. She was devastated.

That shouldn't surprise her. Right from the beginning he had pulled a formidable response from her.

She fought tears as she set out her gown and did her hair, then her makeup, saying a private *Thanks, Trella*, as her sister's face appeared in the mirror to bolster her.

She wished now she had brought one of Trella's designs. Her sister's confections tended to have a self-assured cheekiness whereas Angelique's evoked more introspective moods. Hers tonight was wistful and damned if it wasn't *blue*.

A powder blue in silk, sleeveless, but abundant enough in the skirt to move like quicksilver. The bodice was overlaid with mist-like lace that split apart at her naval and fell into a divided overskirt that became a small train. She pinned her hair back from her face, but let it fall in loose waves behind her naked shoulders and painted her lips a meditative pink.

Her earrings were simple drop crystals that caught the light. A velvet choker with a matching stone collared her throat. A panic switch was sewn on the underside. She and her sister often joked about starting their own line of high-end security wear, but they didn't want to tip off anyone that they wore it themselves.

Just for a moment, as she took in her reflection, she wondered what it would be like to live without so much vigilance. In a prince's harem, for instance.

This lipstick really emphasized the pout she couldn't seem to shake. *Ugh*.

She gathered her composure before facing the masses. It was better that Kasim wasn't with her, she consoled herself. Events like this, when her presence was advertised ahead of time, were always particularly rabid attention-wise. Maurice wore special sunglasses to deal with the glare off the flashbulbs it was so bad.

Maurice was reading something on his phone when she came out the door. He tucked it away promptly, but took it out again when they were in the elevator, since they were alone.

"Je m'excuse," he said. "It's a report about some photos that have surfaced. I'm sending instructions to question their authenticity."

She dismissed his concern with a flick of her brows. "Of me with the prince?"

"It says 'prince,' yes, but—"

"I don't care," she insisted, even though she cared a great deal.

The elevator stopped, the doors opened and some models joined them. One was beyond thrilled to be sharing an elevator with One of The Sauveterre Twins. Maurice put his phone away and remained alert while Angelique exchanged a few remarks with the strangers and consented to a selfie.

Moments later, the doors opened onto the ballroom floor. The paparazzi went mad as soon as they saw she had arrived.

Maurice guided Angelique down the narrow pathway toward the VIP entrance where greeters would be waiting to check off her name on a tablet and handlers would hand her a swag bag that she invariably gave to her mother.

As she approached, a man in a tuxedo turned to look at her.

Kasim.

He was asking if she'd already entered the ballroom when the madness behind him made him turn.

She was stunning. Like an ethereal creature surrounded by fireflies as a million flashbulbs went off behind her.

Even more riveting than her beauty, however, was

the way her composed features softened with surprise, then dawned into warm recognition. Her eyes sparkled and a joyous glow suffused her. Her breasts rose as he moved toward her.

He caught his own breath. Him. The man who had decided this affair was too inconsequential to mention to his father, merely stating he had, indeed, resolved the situation with Sadiq's "friend." While he'd been so far away from her, he'd been able to convince himself their time together had been merely a pleasant diversion.

Nevertheless, he'd found himself bulldozing his way through his meetings, working late to negotiate agreements and pushing hard for resolution, a mental clock urging him to leave on time to be here with her. He had worked nonstop on the plane, barely sparing a moment to put on his tuxedo before finalizing a few last details over the phone in his car, arriving at the perfect moment to watch her emerge from the gauntlet.

Bulbs were still flashing as she unconsciously posed, awaiting his approach with that beautiful, reverent look on her face. He wondered what his looked like. Irritated and possessive, he imagined, since he wanted to steal her away from this madhouse. *Now.*

Mindful of her flawless appearance, he held back on crushing her even though he ached to feel her against him. Instead, he took her hand and detoured past her lips to press a light kiss to her cheekbone.

Her lashes fluttered closed and she breathed, "I'm so glad you're here."

He almost didn't hear her, but the blush that stained her cheeks told him she'd said it and was adorably self-conscious for having revealed herself like that.

"Are you?" He straightened to bask in her look of adoration. "Because I think we've been found out."

Behind her, the paparazzi had moved to completely block the passage. They had become a wall of strobing light and a din of clicks and whirs and shouts of her name.

"Is there anyone else here?" Angelique blinked her green, green eyes, mouth quirking with irony. "I only see you."

"You're stealing my lines." Stealing something else if he wasn't very careful. "Let's get this evening over with so I can have you to myself."

They created a huge stir and for once she didn't care. She was proud, so delighted and proud, to stand beside this man. He was *here*. It wasn't the most important occasion of her life, but it was important to her that he had made an effort.

He *wanted* to be with her.

Although, that could change if the attention didn't lighten up. Kasim might not be as infamous as she was, but with those features, the camera had to love him. His air of detachment meant eyes followed him with a yearning for scraps of his notice.

"You weren't exaggerating about the attention," he said when she returned to her seat after her presentation and he rose to help her with her chair.

"No," she agreed, then had to tease, "Scared?"

"Pah!" he dismissed.

They were an "it" couple before the final speeches had wrapped. "Kasimelique," one of her colleagues teased her in a whisper as the trays of champagne began circulating and the networking portion of the evening began.

"I'm so glad to have that over with," Angelique said to Kasim once they had the first rush of introductions over with and were able to move into a quieter corner for a moment alone. "Did I sound all right when I was onstage?"

"Perfect. You weren't nervous, were you? You didn't look it."

"I told you, my trick is to pretend I'm Trella. Do you know that man?" She tried not to sound so keyed up as she flicked her glance to the right, but this crush of people was wearing on her. "The blond one with the sash," she clarified.

The stranger was tall and quite handsome with a regal bearing. He wore the red satin as a bold streak across his chest beneath his jacket.

"He keeps looking this way. Maybe he's related to a client, but I can't place him. I'm going to be so embarrassed if he comes over and I don't know his name." The Champagne probably wasn't a good idea, but she took a sip anyway. This was still her first glass.

"I don't know who he is, but I recognize the look." Kasim seemed to stand taller and more alert. He took a half step closer to her.

"What do you mean? Like, Nordic heritage? Or do you mean you know the sash?" She lowered her glass, smile fading as she read the suspicion in the way he looked down his nose at her.

"I mean possessive. He's resentful of my place beside you. *Jealous.*"

"Are you serious?" She tried a laugh, but realized very quickly that Kasim was more than serious. He was trying to see inside her head.

"Kasim." She was deeply offended. "I swear to you, I don't know him." But she could see the reel of her online exploits playing behind his eyes.

"Believe what you want," she said frostily. *Don't*

you dare, she silently railed, heart clutched in a vise. He didn't trust her? After all they'd shared?

Well, honestly, what *had* they shared? A weekend of sex and not even some long-distance afterplay via text.

She looked at him with new eyes, thinking of how much she had anticipated his meeting her here, but now she had to wonder if she wasn't simply a convenient booty call. It was so lowering, she had to remind herself to breathe.

"Excuse me." He walked away into the throng, leaving her staring at his disappearing back, confounded and trying not to panic. That was *it*? He had just broken off their affair because a stranger looked at her in a way he didn't like?

Before she could fully absorb that and succumb to fury or despondency or both, the stark white of a truly beautiful tuxedo parked itself before her. It was cut by the slash of red and there was a star-shaped pin at his shoulder with a shield inside it.

The man could have come out of a fairy tale, he was so patrician and perfectly hewn.

She hated him on sight and wanted to throw her champagne in his face, but he spoke with an exotic accent and impeccable manners.

"Your lost item, Cinderella." He offered her a cupped hand.

Inside it was a gold hoop earring with a line of diamonds down the front. It looked exactly like a pair she owned. They'd been a gift from her father for her fifteenth birthday—not something run-of-the-mill that showed up in every low-budget jewelry shop. Trella's were similar, but that one was definitely the match to her own.

She took it to examine it more closely, trying to recall when she'd worn them last.

"Where—?"

"Caught under the pill—" he started to say in a tone that was very throaty with latent passion, but he cut himself off. Something in his expression grew sharp and arrested as he studied her face. Whatever lightness might have been in his mood became something accusatory as his gaze moved restlessly over her like he was searching for something he couldn't find.

She knew that look, but refused to believe she was interpreting it correctly. It was far too outrageous to imagine—

"I knew if I walked away, he would approach you," Kasim said, reappearing beside her.

Angelique startled, not exactly guilty, but defensive. *No.* She needed time to figure out what was going on with this stranger. She searched his blue eyes, now distinctly frosted with hostility toward Kasim. *And* her.

Kasim's gaze cut to the earring in her hand, making her close her fist around it.

"Introduce us." Kasim's tone was lethal.

Angelique was distantly aware of people sidling by them, glancing their way.

Kasim's expression was positively murderous and this stranger was shifting his gaze from her to Kasim, contempt curling his lip.

"I told you," she insisted to Kasim in an undertone. "I don't know him."

Trella, you didn't.

"My timing is inconvenient," the stranger said, flicking a look to Kasim that was a silent warning. *Be careful with this one.*

It was so infuriatingly *male*, like they were lofty

equals who came across tarts like her all the time, she instantly wanted to smack him. Both of them. How dare he show up and throw her under the bus this way. How dare he touch her sister! Her heart began to race, trying to assimilate how it could possibly have happened.

Was she crazy? Could he have been with Trella? How? *When?*

At the same time she was trying to work it out, she could see she was dropping like a free fall elevator in Kasim's estimation. That *hurt*, damn it. How could he think this of her?

"If you're going to accuse me of being a slut, at least tell me who you are," she bit out.

"You picked that label," the stranger shot back derisively. "And I don't *care* that you've moved on, but those are real diamonds. I was going to send it by courier back to Paris, but I read that you were going to be here and I was in Berlin." He shrugged a dismissal, looking distinctly bored as he glanced away. "My mistake. Carry on."

But he stood there like he was waiting for Kasim to give up and leave, as if he wanted to continue talking to her.

"*Back* to Paris," she repeated, reclaiming the stranger's attention while hotly aware that Kasim was glancing away as though looking for an exit. "When exactly was I there with you? Wait. Let me guess," she insisted, because it finally hit her. It was completely impossible, but she *knew*. "Last Friday night? The charity dinner for the Brighter Days Children's Foundation?"

The stranger's cheeks went hollow. "You know it was."

"Kasim, where was I last weekend? *All* weekend?"

Finally she had his attention. His resentful, derisive attention.

"You *are* both aware I have a twin. *Aren't you?*"

Kasim couldn't say that he was relieved when Angelique cleared herself of cheating on him. He was still too gripped by residual possessiveness. Maybe his jealous rage had eased enough that he was capable of rational thought, maybe he'd ceased wanting to *kill* the other man acting so proprietarily toward Angelique, but he was still pulsing with adrenaline. The sheer force of emotion that had overtaken him as he identified a rival was paralyzing.

Unnerving.

"I'll need your name and contact details," Angelique said while signaling Maurice to approach.

"His Highness, Xavier Deunoro," Kasim supplied stiffly. "Prince of Elazar."

Angelique and the prince both turned raised-brow looks his way.

Kasim shrugged. "I asked when I walked away."

"Another prince. *Charming,*" Angelique said scathingly.

Upset that he'd been mistrustful? She should look at the facts before him: they hadn't been together all week, her sister was never in public and this man had brought her damned earring from what was no doubt his *bed*. Shared intimacy was the only reason he would want to return it personally.

"She said she was you," the prince said as he reached to an inside pocket of his tuxedo. "The resemblance is remarkable, but there is something…" He narrowed his eyes. "I can't put my finger on it, but the moment I saw you tonight, I knew something was different."

That made Angelique stiffen and flash a wary glance at the man, but she recovered quickly and took the prince's card, relaying it to her guard with a hand that shook.

"That explains the photos you were questioning," she said to Maurice. "My brothers will want that, but wait until I've spoken to Trella. I'll head upstairs to do that now." With a hard glance at her sister's lover, she said, "If you tell anyone it was her and not me, I will personally hunt you down and unman you." She looked as gloriously provocative as she had the day Kasim had met her.

"You can try," the prince drawled. "Give her my regards."

Angelique turned away only to be confronted by a Hollywood starlet.

"I'm sorry," Angelique said with tested graciousness, briefly clasping the actress's hand. "I've been called away. I'm looking forward to our appointment next month, though. We'll talk then."

"My people will need a copy of the press release before it's sent," Kasim said, taking out his phone as he fell into step with her, winding toward the nearest exit.

"What press release?"

"The one clarifying her identity."

"That won't happen."

He checked briefly, not faced with any physical obstructions, but walking into the wall of his own ego.

"You will," he informed her. "Or I will."

"Do not make threats in that direction, Kasim."

"It's not a threat. It's a statement. I can't allow people to have a wrong impression." His father would find Kasim's means of putting Sadiq's problem to bed rather crude as it was.

"After what you just thought about me, you might be surprised how little I care about how this reflects on *you*. I would rather the general public think the worst of me than know the truth, however."

"Why?" he demanded.

"Reasons."

They approached the melee of reporters. He was forced to table his questions as they pushed their way through the chaos to the elevators.

Her guard efficiently plowed them a way and barred anyone from coming into the car with them, but Angelique still had the gall to look at Kasim like he was a hitchhiker who had hopped on from the highway.

"I'm going to my room to call my sister. You're not invited," she said.

"It's my room," he stated.

She shot a look to Maurice who was instantly alarmed. "That shouldn't happen," her guard said, reaching for his phone. "I'll call—"

"I know the owners," Kasim said tightly. "I pulled strings to take over the reservation. It's *fine*."

"It really isn't." Angelique sailed out the doors as they opened, striding down the hall with her elegant dress trailing behind her like a visible whorl of her cloud of fury.

One of Kasim's own guards had joined Maurice's partner at the door to the suite, leaving Kasim's bag just inside on the floor. Angelique gave both a baleful look and walked straight through the lounge into the bedroom where she quickly shut the door. Seconds later Kasim heard the dull ring of her placing a call and a greeting in a muted voice that held a tone that sounded much like her own.

He took out his own phone and searched for the most

recent photos of Angelique Sauveterre. Most were from tonight, first the ones of them greeting each other outside the ballroom, then mingling within. A few showed her onstage, and one grainy snap across the restaurant last weekend was obviously a belated effort to pile on tonight's revelation that they were dating.

Then there were a handful of images that showed her—it damned well looked *exactly* like her—in a clinch with the Prince of Elazar in a ballroom in Paris.

And someone had managed to snap her very tense expression as she had defended herself against two-timing right before they'd come up here.

Kasim gritted his teeth as he weighed Sauveterre security protocols against his own reputation. He could spare Angelique an hour to address this scandal in her own way, he allowed generously. After that, he would turn down the heat on this particular conflagration himself.

Twenty minutes later, Angelique emerged from the bedroom, cheeks flushed, brows pulled into a distraught line. Opening the door, she said, "Maurice, can you send a snapshot of that card I gave you to Trella? *Merci*."

She closed the door firmly and turned to glare at Kasim.

"Does she do this often?" Kasim asked.

She pursed her lips as though deciding whether to answer. Then she huffed out a breath and crossed her arms defensively, but her shoulders fell a notch.

"It's something she's tried a few times in the last year, basically since she knew Sadiq was getting married. She wants to attend the wedding and is determined to get over…" She stopped herself. Sighed again. "It's a way for her to test the waters of moving in public again. If she appeared as herself, the press would go stark raving mad. If she poses as me, however, and goes to Ramon's race with Henri and Cinnia or something like that, it's run-of-the-mill attention."

Tonight was run-of-the-mill?

"Shouldn't she get it over with? Coming out at my sister's wedding is liable to take attention away from the bride and groom. Has she thought of that?"

"It will be a closed ceremony and don't judge how she's doing this."

"Her actions deserve to be judged. I look like a fool. If you had had an actual affair with that man last *year*, I wouldn't care." That was a small lie, but he would be able to convince himself he didn't care. "The fact you've been photographed with both of us in the same week makes all three of us look bad."

"We're all going to have to grin and bear it, aren't we?"

"No," he told her sternly. "You warned me about attention. You didn't say your sister would ridicule me. I will give her the chance to come clean. If she doesn't, I will make the completely true statement that you were with me in London all of last weekend."

"No!" Her fists hit the air next to her thighs, arms straight and angry. "Don't *do* that to her."

"I didn't take the photographs, Angelique. She's bringing this on herself!"

"It could do so much damage, you can't even comprehend." She paced with agitation across the lounge. "The press was horrible to her for years after the kidnapping, printing every lurid scrap, fact or fiction, on what happened while she was captive. True or not, those things assaulted her every time, victimizing her again and again. Then, as if that wasn't bad enough, they called her unstable and a drug addict and *fat*. She was barely a stone heavier than me, but there was this magnifying glass on her so she couldn't buy a stick of gum without it being a cry for help, or a sign she was suicidal… It drove her to go the other way, until she was underweight and we were scared she would disappear completely. I'll tell you, if anything is designed to break a person's spirit, it's that sort of relentless, vicious criticism."

She paused to take a few panting breaths. Her face contorted in a wince of distant memory.

"Then, after my father's funeral… I guess we finally looked like young women by then. It's not like we were dressed for clubbing, you know, but photos circulated of us at the service and men stalked both of us online after that, saying the most disgusting things. Sending us—" She waved a hand toward her crotch. "*Those* sorts of pics. It was even worse for Trella. She knew what men like that are capable of." Her voice broke on the last words, eyes haunted.

"Angelique," he breathed, and started toward her.

She bent to unfasten her shoes and kick them away, then kept moving, restless with heightened emotion, dress swirling like a cape each time she turned.

"She started having panic attacks because of it. That is *not* public knowledge." She pointed at him as though warning him not to speak of it. Then she whirled away again. "She was terrified all the time. It was horrible for her. For all of us. It was like watching someone who is depressed to the point of being suicidal, or in chronic pain, and listening to them scream. You can't do anything except sit there and watch. She spent, God, a good two years stoned on medications, trying to get it under control. Finally she left the public eye and it took a while, but she was able to stabilize. That was so hard-won, none of us rocks the boat. We don't want to throw her off again."

She hugged herself, gaze fixed on the past.

"For years, one of us has always been with her, never farther than the next room. We all know it's not healthy. We *want* a normal life for her. Our version of normal, anyway," she muttered, then waved with exasperation toward the guards in the hall.

"Even Trella is balking at how she lives. I just asked her how this happened and she told me she feels like she's been doing time on a prison sentence for a crime she didn't commit. What did she do wrong, Kasim? Are her kidnappers half so tortured? They might be in jail, but have they suffered one-tenth as much as she has? And even through all of what she has faced, she *tries*."

Her eyes were wet and gleaming. She was visibly shaking with intense emotion, making his heart feel pinched and tight.

"She's been trying so hard to get over all her mental blocks. She flew to Paris alone. You have no idea what a big deal that was for her. And then, when she realized you and I were keeping out of the spotlight and I was expected at that dinner, she stole the chance to go out as me. To see how she felt going out *alone*. It was a spur-of-the moment thing, which is exactly like her when she's at her best. In certain ways this is such thrilling news."

She began pacing again, her dress flaring around her as she pivoted, but halted to press a hand to her brow.

"Not the part where she went home with a stranger, of course. I asked her how *that* happened, but she didn't want to talk about it, only apologized for not telling him who she really was. My brothers are going to kill me for not being there to stop her."

Kasim folded his arms, observing drily, "She took acting like you to the highest level, didn't she?"

Angelique jerked her head up, eyes narrowed with antipathy. "I had dinner with you first!"

They hadn't even finished their drinks, let alone started on the appetizers, but *okay*.

"That has to be me in those photos, Kasim. If the press gets wind that it was her…" She pinched the bridge of her nose. "Trella is a tiny baby sea turtle making her way to the water. If we can just give her time to get there before unleashing the crabs and gulls…"

He snorted. "Laying it on pretty thick, aren't you?"

"What do you want me to say? That it's okay if you traumatize my sister by causing the hell of public attention to rain down on her again? It's not."

"What do you want *me* to say? That it's okay if the world thinks you've slept with both of us? It's *not*."

"Who cares so long as you're the one in this room with me tonight? Or, wait, am I invited to stay in the room I booked for myself?"

He scowled. "Don't get bent out of shape about that. I don't book weekends with women then ask them to foot the bill."

"I see. That's interesting." She gave a considering nod, shoulders setting in a stiff line. "You realize that by mentioning these legions of other women for whom you have paid hotel bills, you're saying it's okay that you have a past, but not me. Is that what you were doing this week, by the way? When you were not texting me? Paying for hotel rooms with other women? Just because no one returned a cuff link downstairs doesn't mean you weren't making a fool of *me*, but do you hear me complaining? No. Because I'm well aware we haven't made any commitments to each other—"

"Enough," he cut in. "I paid for the room because I will put up with your pain-in-the-ass security protocols, but you will stay in *my* room. I will not ask permission from *your* guards to enter. As for the photos, I don't want people to think that's you because I'm jealous. All right? Is that what you need to hear?"

Her shoulders went back, but he could see he had finally pulled her out of her own interests into *theirs*.

"Which I might have hesitated to admit if you weren't acting like a green-eyed shrew yourself. No, Angelique, I was not sleeping with other women. I was working. Nonstop. So I could come here and be with you. Future or not, we are damned well exclusive to one another until we're over. Is that clear? Now, go warn your sister I won't be so forgiving if she does this to me again."

The line of her mouth softened. "You're not going to expose her?"

"Do I look like someone who takes pleasure in feeding baby sea turtles to the gulls?"

She threw herself at him.

CHAPTER EIGHT

ANGELIQUE GLIMPSED THE velvet box on the romantically set table when she arrived at Kasim's Paris penthouse.

She was getting to know him very well, but wouldn't have pegged him as a man who celebrated a one-month anniversary. His sentimentalism touched her. It told her he valued what they had as deeply as she did.

"We're staying in tonight?" she asked as she kissed him without even taking off her jacket or setting down her purse.

He had already shed his suit jacket and tasted faintly of Scotch and…tension? He lingered over their kiss, drawing it out with a quest for her response, waiting until they were both breathless and hot before drawing back.

"Do you mind?"

"No." She tossed her purse toward the sofa then hugged her arms around his waist again. Nestled her mons into his hardness, pleased with the evidence his desire wasn't letting up any more than hers. "It's been a long week. I missed you. I'd rather have you all to myself."

"Me, too." His voice was sincere, but…off. He started to pull her into another kiss.

She hesitated. "Are you angry?"

A flash in his eyes, then, "Not at you."

He combed his fingers into her hair and gently pinned her head back, so her neck was arched, her chin tilted up for the press of his damp lips. The stamp of hot kisses went down her throat, making her skin tighten and tingle.

"And you can't talk about it so you want to forget it. Perhaps I can help with that," she allowed with another press of her hips into his groin. It was her cross to bear that she was the lover of a man with great responsibilities.

His breath hissed in and he straightened to his full height, seeming to wage an inner debate. He bit out a soft curse and his hands fell away from her.

"We will have to talk about it," he said, twirling his finger to indicate she should turn and let him help her with her coat. "Much as I'd rather make love to you first, you probably wouldn't forgive me if I did. Let's get it over with."

Wary now, she watched him drape her jacket over the back of the sofa and move to the chilled wine in the bucket.

"A votre santé," she said when he brought her a glass.

He only made a face of dismay and said bluntly, "You can't come to the wedding."

Angelique held the wine in her mouth until it was warm and sour. She swallowed.

"Sadiq and Hasna's wedding?" *Obviously*, but she couldn't process how he could say such a thing. "I know we can't...be together when I'm there. I wasn't expecting—" To stay in his room. Maybe she'd fantasized about it. "I mean, I thought I'd stay with my family and you and I could..." She shrugged. "Dance?" Steal time somewhere? They were very adept at that.

"My father is inviting the woman he would like me to marry. It would be awkward and disrespectful for my mistress to be there."

And the hits just kept on coming.

His marriage was supposed to be some far-off thing that would happen one day, but in the mists of a distant future, like death. Unavoidable, but not something the average person worried about as an immediate concern.

"Did you explain my family's relationship with Sadiq?" Her hand began to shake. She leaned to set her glass on the coffee table before she spilled wine all over his antique Persian rug.

"My father is still convinced you had a personal relationship with him. Bringing up the complimentary wardrobe does more harm than good."

"I'm not going to miss Sadiq's wedding, Kasim. He asked us to be there. It's a big deal for all of us, especially if Trella is going to be with us. I have to be there for *her*."

"I'm not happy about it either, but it's *one* day."

"Does Hasna know?"

"I'm not about to play those sorts of politics," he said, sharp and hard. "That is my mother's game, to stir up tears to manipulate my father. Hasna understands our father very well along with my promise to marry the wife he chooses for me."

"Why—?" Why had he ever agreed to such a thing? But she knew. So he could rule differently. Better.

That selflessness on his part ought to inspire her to make peace here and act in the greater good, but she was too appalled at how casually and callously he was brushing aside her feelings in this.

He set down his wine and grasped her arms. "Angelique, it's one day. Then we can carry on as normal."

"Normal being this." She broke away from his hold to wave at the room.

The impermanence of their association penetrated. What she had seen as a relationship, one where she could reveal her deepest thoughts and worries, was nothing more than a convenience for him.

She caught sight of the table and its narrow velvet box. Its significance struck like a bludgeon.

"Silly me, I thought that was for our anniversary," she said dumbly.

"Anni—?" He pinned his lips shut. Such a man. One hundred percent oblivious.

She walked around the far end of the sofa and moved to open the box.

The necklace was a stunning confection of thin chains and cushion-cut emeralds set in gold.

This was all she would be left with when their affair was over. Some token of his. It wasn't even affection, was it? Appreciation? For the orgasms she'd given him?

And this affair *would* end. She had managed to ignore that reality these past few weeks of meeting him in hotel rooms across Europe.

He was marrying. Sooner than later. And his chosen wife would be at the wedding.

It was absolutely true that she couldn't meet that woman then carry on with Kasim until… When? The day his engagement was announced? Days before he married? Her heart was pulsing like a raw wound just thinking of it.

Each breath she drew felt like a conscious effort and burned both directions. In and out. Her throat closed and her eyes swam. Her voice came out strained with insult.

"I'm not a woman you buy off, Kasim."

She looked up in time to see him flinch and avert his gaze.

"I know you're disappointed," he began. "That is not—"

She cut him off with a hoot of disbelief. "Is that what I am? *Disappointed?*" Her chest was caving in on itself. "Are *you?*"

"It's *one* day."

"It's you turning me into your mistress, then letting your father call me a whore who's not good enough to be seen in his palace. One who is paid well, I admit, but no thanks. I'm not interested." She gave the velvet box a thrust of rejection so it tipped off the table onto the floor.

"You're overreacting," he bit out, trying to catch the necklace.

"No, *you* should have told me this could happen before you took me to your bed! That is information I needed because you know what Sadiq means to us."

"And what? You would have passed on all of this so you could attend one damned wedding?"

"All of what?" she charged, waving at the necklace he now held. "You've just reduced our relationship to an exchange of sex for jewelry. Do you know what I've given up so I could be with you? The sacrifices I've made? I've pushed Trella *away* so I could be close to you. What have you given up? *Nothing.* And now I know why. Because I mean nothing to you. So, yes, the wedding is a deal breaker. Tell your father your mistress won't be there because you no longer have one."

She turned toward her coat.

He caught her arm. "Angelique—"

"Don't," she said in the deadly, assertive voice she'd been trained to use, free hand snatching up her pendant in warning.

His mouth tightened and he lifted his hand to splay it in the air, like she'd turned a gun on him.

"Really? You'll call in your guards rather than have a civilized conversation about this?"

"How do you see this conversation ending? In your bed? Yes, I will call in my guards rather than let you seduce me into accepting this kind of treatment. You had chances to end this before my—" *Don't say "heart."*

"Before my emotions were involved." Her voice shook. "Did you really think, after all that I've shared with you, that I was only here for a *necklace*?"

The control that she had cultivated through a lifetime of having to buck up and be strong was never harder to find. She shot her arms into her coat and picked up her purse.

"You're as emotionally tone-deaf as your father."

If she had been trying to stab him in the heart, she had picked up the most efficient knife with which to do the job, then snapped it off against the bone for good measure.

As he gathered the necklace from the floor, he thought of Jamal showing it to him a decade ago. It was one of his brother's first efforts at a big piece, not perfect, designed with more passion than attention to the finer details, but it was genuinely beautiful. Jamal had been rightfully proud and Kasim sincerely impressed.

Kasim had bought it, wanting to be his brother's first patron, declaring, *Someday it will be worn by a queen, as it should be.*

But lately, as he regularly saw green and gold tones in the eyes of his lover when she woke beside him, he had decided to give it to Angelique. He had known she wouldn't like what he had to say today, but he had hoped to soften the blow by giving her something that was genuinely precious to him, that was hard to give up because it was one of the few remnants of his brother he had.

Of course she wasn't aware of that. There had been no point in trying to explain. He had let the door slam and the quiet set like concrete around him.

Because they had no future. His father was choosing him a wife. The goal today had been to keep her from attending the wedding and that task was definitely accomplished.

Sometimes hard choices had to be made. Jamal had been one of them and Angelique another.

It made him furious and sick, but it was done.

Angelique heard the door, but didn't get out of bed. She was too devastated. Her eyes were swollen and gritty, her throat raw, her nose congested and her heart sitting in a line of jagged pieces behind her breastbone.

She had tried to brave it out on her own, but sometime in the darkest hours of the night, when her sister had texted, asking if she was all right, her willpower had collapsed.

Please come, she had texted.

Trella hadn't asked why. She had only texted back that she would leave as soon as the family jet could be cleared for takeoff. Now her sister's shoulders fell as she walked into the bedroom and took in the shipwreck that was her twin.

"What happened?" Trella asked gently.

"We broke up," Angelique said in a voice rasped by hours of crying. "I've been so stupid."

"No." Trella came to the bed and swept away the crumpled tissues to lie down in front of her. "You fell in love. That's not stupid." She stroked Angelique's hair back from where it was stuck to her wet cheek.

"I didn't mean to." Fresh tears flooded her eyes. "I never let anyone in. You know I don't. It's too painful."

"You were always so full of my suffering there was no room for anyone else."

"No."

"Yes, Gili." Trella stroked her hair, petting and soothing. "I tried not to put it on you, but you carry it because that's who you are. I'm not surprised you fell for him when he was the first person who didn't lean on you emotionally. When you finally felt like I didn't need you every minute. That must have felt like such a relief."

"He didn't lean on me because he didn't love me!" Angelique pushed a fresh tissue under her nose and sniffed. "And I feel so pathetic, crying like this when a bruised heart is nothing compared to—"

"Shh…" Trella said, stroking her hair. "Don't ever compare, *bebé* angel."

Angelique closed her eyes and tried to level out her breathing. "I thought I had learned how to be strong and I'm so…" *Sad. Scorned. Heartbroken.*

"Do you know how I get through my worst moments?" Trella's fingers gently wove in and picked up Angelique's hair, combing to the ends. Her voice was pitched into the tone they had used as children, when telling each other secrets in the night. "Every time I've wanted to give up, I've always thought to myself, I have to be there when *she* needs *me*. You gave me a gift, asking me to come. You're telling me I'm strong enough to be your support. It was worth fighting through all that I have so I could be with you here, in your hour."

Angelique had seen her begging Trella to come as pure weakness, but wondered now if she had failed to see what a comeback her sister was really making— because she'd been so wrapped up in Kasim.

"You didn't hesitate, even though I've been letting him come between us." Her lips quivered and she looked at her twin through matted lashes. "That was wrong. I'm so sorry."

"No," Trella crooned. "Don't apologize for offering your heart to him. It's his loss that he didn't see how tender and precious it is. And no matter what happens, we will always be us. I *will* be here for you, Gili."

Angelique's smile wobbled and she let out a breath she'd been holding for years. "I love you, Trella *bella*."

"I love you, too."

Angelique wasn't going to Zhamair. She wasn't buckling to Kasim's demand that she stay away, though. It was the other way. She couldn't bear to see him, fearing she would make a fool of herself at the first glance.

Or, at the very least, have to face what a fool she already was.

She had always seen easily through men who asked her out. They wanted to date her because she was beautiful, a prize. Some had wanted to get closer to her brothers, others had been so overcome in her presence it had been a burden to live up to what they imagined her to be. It had been fairly easy to maintain a certain distance.

Kasim had been different. He was strong, confident, *honest*. She had felt safe with him and it had allowed her to put her true self out to him. That inner soul of hers was as shy and hesitant as she'd ever been, only coming out when she trusted she wouldn't be hurt.

Yet he had treated her like one more mare in the stable and she should have seen it coming, which left her feeling like she'd set herself up for this heartache. She had failed herself.

Be the tough woman Trella is, she kept urging herself, but she had never managed to be that woman when it came to Kasim. That was her downfall.

So she finished drafting her email to Sadiq mentioning the "terrible flu" that had her deeply under the weather and hit Send.

She was fooling no one. Her family knew that things were over between her and Kasim. Hasna had to be aware of it, as well.

She sniffed and glanced at her red eyes in her desk mirror. She certainly looked like she was battling a serious ailment. Heartsickness took a toll.

Trella, bless her, was doing everything she could to support her.

It was the great reversal Angelique had longed for and it wasn't nearly as relieving or satisfying as she'd imagined. For starters, her brothers looked at her reliance on Trella as a small betrayal of their unspoken pact. They had all worn the mantle of protector for so long, they couldn't put it down long enough to see that Angelique's pulling back had actually been a good thing for their baby sister.

Trella was stepping up on her own volition now. She had planned to attend the wedding, but it was her suggestion that she take on the wedding day with Hasna so Angelique could skip going to Zhamair. This morning, Trella had even volunteered to make a quick run to London *by herself* to meet in private with a certain longtime client who belonged to the royal family and had a confidential occasion coming up.

Trella was also talking of doing more of the front end work once she returned from Zhamair, which was something to look forward to, but for now the task of greeting prospective clients still fell on Angelique.

Thus, when her guard rang from the front doors, stating that her eleven o'clock was here, she could only sigh and agree to come downstairs.

As she rose, she glanced at the appointment details. Girard Pascal. Something about a gift for a bride. Since she had no other reference on this prospective client, he would be shown into the small receiving room off the front foyer.

The room was a quaint little conversation area filled with Queen Anne furniture that served as a border crossing of sorts. Technically inside the building, it was still on the perimeter. Staff and accepted clients went through a second controlled door to enter the hallowed interior.

The reception room had two doors and a window onto the foyer, giving the illusion of a more spacious chamber, but the glass was really there to allow the guards to monitor her safety if the doors happened to be closed.

Girard Pascal looked Arabic, that was her first impression, but there were many Parisians with Middle Eastern heritage who had been here for generations. With that name, she assumed he was French.

He looked like Kasim, was her second thought, as he stood to a height that was very close to her former lover's. The resemblance was only in his coloring and ancestry, she told herself. Maybe something indefinable across his cheekbones. His eyes, too. That bottom lip. His build and the commanding way he held himself.

She ignored the leap of her heart and told herself she

was making more of the superficial similarities because she missed Kasim. That was all.

Then he opened his mouth and spoke with the same accent, almost the same tone and intonation. "Please call me Girard. Thank you for seeing me."

He smiled warmly, looking nervous in a way that she almost thought was male attraction, but it wasn't. Nor was it the fan-based giddiness some people showed in meeting a Sauveterre. It was affection and admiration and a searching of her expression for something she couldn't define.

"I'm Angelique. Please sit and tell me what sort of gift you had in mind. If I can't help you, I'm sure I'll be able to suggest someone who can." It was her stock greeting, something to give her an out if she decided not to take on a client.

She was already leaning toward not. She didn't feel threatened, precisely, but she did feel prevailed upon. He wanted something from her. Not just a spring ensemble, either.

He held up a finger and went to the door, waiting while one of her guards brought over a black pouch smaller than his palm.

"Nothing showed on the X-ray. It's fine," her guard told her.

"Do you mind?" Girard said as he stepped back into the room and started to close the door.

Angelique moved to close the second door, then joined him at the coffee table, sitting in the opposite armchair from his.

"My request is very…" He frowned, searching for words, then poured out the contents of the pouch onto the coffee table.

It was a necklace, the chain three delicate strands of

white gold, the pendant complex and simple at once. The stones were blue, set into a graceful sweep that almost looked like a cursive letter.

"Arabic?" she guessed, caught by both its whimsy and the suggestion of joy.

"It means 'with.'" His smile flashed.

"It's beautiful." She was instantly taken by it and moved to the settee so she could examine it more closely.

"May I?" She reached out, adding in a murmur, "You want me to design something to go with it?" She would love to. The well of her creativity began to burble just feeling the weight of the piece against her fingers. It had a certain magic that penetrated her skin right into her blood.

"I believe you already have."

"Pardon?" She dragged her stunned gaze off the crimping on the claws, experiencing a shiver as she recognized the workmanship. "Did you make something for my brother, Henri? A tennis bracelet with pink and white diamonds?"

"I don't discuss my clients." His mouth twitched as if he knew that she'd said that same thing more times than she could count. "But my work is carried by a jeweler here in Paris and one in London. And I did make something like that when I first moved to France. It's quite possible the bracelet is mine."

"I meant to ask him where he got it," she murmured, but her brother wasn't speaking to her, primarily because she had dared to invade the family flat and discovered that Cinnia had left him. "I would love to work together," she blurted. "I'm bowled over by your skill."

He smiled with shy pleasure, eyes gleaming. "That touches me. You can't imagine how much. But let me ask my favor first. Then we'll see what you think of working with me on something else."

"Yes, right. Did you see a piece of mine somewhere? You know it's just as likely designed by Trella?" She looked at the pendant again, trying to imagine how she could have inspired something so beautiful. She was utterly in love with it.

"I made this for my sister. I was hoping you could take it to her."

"Your— Oh, my God!" If she hadn't been so enthralled with the necklace, she would have put it together sooner. Now she quickly dropped the pendant on the table and jerked to her feet, backing away from a ghost. "Oh, my God!"

Charles shot in.

She held up her hand.

"I'm fine. Just a shock," she insisted to her guard. "What is today's word? I can't even remember. Daffodil?" She touched her forehead. "Honestly, I'm fine. I just need a moment with…"

She waved at *Kasim's dead brother*. Her hand trembled.

"I'm so sorry," Jamal said with a wince. "I thought you might know."

"How—? *No*." She had to be white as a sheet, but managed to shoo Charles out.

He continued to watch her closely through the glass.

"Oh, my God, Jamal," she breathed. "How on earth would I know? Your whole family thinks you're dead." She held her hand to her throat where she felt her own pulse thundering like a bullet train.

"Kasim didn't tell you? He helped arrange it. The death certificate and name change…"

"No he didn't tell me!" It caused her quite a pang to

admit it, but she had already processed that however much she had thought she meant to Kasim, she had actually meant a lot less.

"Good God, *why*?" She moved to the settee and sank down, wilting as the shock wore off and her mind jammed with questions. "I mean, he told me that your father didn't like that you were an artist, but—"

"Is that what he said?" His smile was crooked and poignant. "Our father couldn't accept that I was *gay*."

"Oh," she breathed. More secrets with which Kasim hadn't trusted her. She had been so open about her own family. It made her feel so callow to think of it. Where had her precious speech gone? The one from her first dinner with Kasim, when she had told him she was reticent out of respect for her siblings. But had he entrusted her with Jamal's story? *No.*

"You couldn't just…live in exile? Here?" she asked.

"My lover was already here and beaten to within an inch of his life for…leading me into that life."

"No! Oh, dear God. Your father couldn't have arranged that?"

"People in his government. There are those in Zhamair who are still very prejudiced. They said they were protecting the reputation of the crown, but my father did nothing to prevent or punish them." Deep emotion gripped him for a moment and he struggled to regain his composure, swallowing audibly before continuing. "Either way, I couldn't risk Bernard's life again. I feared for my own. Merely leaving wouldn't have been enough. I was afraid to even see Kasim again, in case it made things difficult for him, or exposed us."

He propped his elbows on his thighs, back bowed with the weight of the world, expression weary. He rubbed his hands over his face, then looked at her over his clasped fingers.

"My mother's life is not easy. The queen is very resentful of her. If my mother had had a gay son living flagrantly abroad…" He shook his head. "No. It was terribly cruel to tell her I was dead, but if the queen picks on her now, my father stands up for her out of respect for her grief."

"I can't imagine," she murmured, appalled anew at the ugly aggression Kasim had grown up in. "I'm so sorry, Jamal."

"Why?" he said, looking and sounding so much like Kasim, her throat tightened. "You had nothing to do with it."

"I wish I could do something, I guess." She realized immediately that she had backed herself into a corner.

His smile was sharp and amused. "Thank you. I would like that."

She shook her head. "You're so much like him it's unnerving. But I can't take that to Hasna and tell her it's from you. You think *I* was shocked!"

"No," he agreed. "She can't know I'm alive, but Kasim could tell her it was in my old collection and that he had been saving it for her wedding day. It would mean a lot to me for her to wear this. I know she would."

"We're not, um… Kasim and I aren't seeing each other anymore." The press hadn't quite caught on, so she wasn't surprised he didn't know. The words still abraded her throat. "I'm not going to Zhamair."

"Ah. I didn't realize." His expression fell. "I'm sorry. From the photos I saw, you both looked quite…" He didn't finish, only looked at the necklace, crestfallen.

She looked at it, too.

With. He wanted to be with his sister in the only way he could.

She couldn't tell this to Trella or one of her brothers. It was Kasim's secret. Jamal's *life.*

I am a sucker, she thought. Trella would have a far better sense of self-protection. Kasim didn't even want her there. She would be an embarrassment. He might even throw her out.

But Jamal looked so disconsolate. And Hasna missed her brother so much. It would mean the world to her to have this...

She closed her eyes, defeated. "I'll go. I'll go to Zhamair and give this to Kasim."

CHAPTER NINE

THERE HAD BEEN many times over the years that Kasim wondered how his father could be such a pitiless, dictatorial bastard. These days, he understood the liberation in such an attitude as he adopted the same demeanor, contemptuous of those around him for being ruled by their emotions. What did the desires of others' egos and libidos and hearts matter when his own had to be ignored? Everyone made sacrifices.

Don't think of her.

Were it not for his sister marrying in *two days*, he would ride into the desert and take some much needed time to regroup. Instead, he was part of a ceaseless revolving door of relatives and dignitaries. One branch of the royal family had no sooner arrived and joined him and his parents for coffee, when a foreign dignitary was in the next room awaiting a chance to express felicitations.

This morning the parade had begun with an ambush. The king had introduced him to the father of the woman he thought would make a fine queen someday—when she grew up. Did his father seriously expect him to marry a child of barely eighteen?

To his prospective father-in-law's credit, a concern for the age difference was expressed. Kasim smoothly stated he could wait until she completed her degree if that was preferred. It would serve the kingdom better if the future queen was well educated.

The king had correctly interpreted it as an effort to put things off and took him to task the minute they were alone.

"Did you give me your word or not?"

"I cleared the field for her, didn't I?" Kasim replied in a similar snarl. A glance over the guest list a few days ago had shown that Angelique had sent her regrets. "Surely we can get one wedding over with before we host the next?"

Sadiq's family were announced, cutting short the clash. Kasim sat down with Sadiq and their fathers to sign off on the marriage contracts, then they joined the queen and Sadiq's mother.

"Hasna isn't here?" Sadiq said, morose as he glanced around the room.

"The gown has arrived," the queen said with a nettled look toward the king. "Fatina has been pestering to see it. Such a nuisance when Hasna has guests. What if she ruins it?"

"The girls will not let that happen," Sadiq's mother soothed. "They have been ever so careful this week, watching the unpacking of Hasna's wardrobe."

"The Sauveterres staying with you?" the queen asked in her most benign yet shrewd tone.

"Oh, yes," Sadiq's mother said with a smile of pleasure. "The men went into the desert for what the Westerners call…a stag? Is that correct, Sadiq? I had a nice visit with their mother. We are all friends for many years."

"And they all came with you here?" the king asked, gaze swinging like a scythe to Kasim. "Both girls?"

"Yes, Trella was the one we worried wouldn't make it, but then Angelique came down with the flu. She recovered, though, and..." Sadiq's mother lost some of her warm cheer as she sensed the growing tension. "Is there a problem?" She touched the draped folds of her hijab where it covered her throat. "I know we said she was not coming, but she shares a room with her sister so I didn't think it would be an imposition when she made it after all?"

"It's no problem," Kasim said firmly, aiming it at his father.

Get rid of her, he read in the flick of his father's imperious glance.

If she had left things as they'd been in Paris, Kasim brooded as he strode down the marbled hall of the palace, he would be resentful, but not furious.

This. This was unacceptable. Now he would be in for it with his father. Threats would be made. His uncle and several cousins were coming to the wedding. Tensions were high. Impulsive autocratic decisions could easily be made in a fit of temper.

Not only was he now courting *that* disastrous possibility, thanks to Angelique coming here against his orders, but he was raw all over again. Her rejection stung afresh and his intense feeling of being hemmed in by impossible circumstances was renewed.

He had resigned himself to never seeing her again, damn her! Now she was *in his home.*

He started to ask a passing servant which suite the Sauveterres had been given, but glimpsed a face he knew down near the end of the hall, standing outside the door to his sister's apartment.

His heart rate spiked as he approached the guard.

"Charles," he said, ears ringing. Angelique was behind this door.

"Your Highness."

Kasim knocked.

Female laughter cut off and his youngest half sister cracked the door to peer out at him. Her smile beamed as she recognized him.

"Kasim!"

"Is Hasna dressed? May I come in?" He fought for a level tone. Distempered as he was, he would never take out his bad mood on a six-year-old.

There was a murmur of female voices, then Hasna called, "Yes, come in."

He entered, picking up his baby sister as he did, kissing her cheek and using her small frame to cushion the rush of emotion that accosted him as he anticipated seeing Angelique.

Hasna's suite was half the size of his, yet still one of the most opulent in the palace, decorated in peacock blues and silver, with high ceilings and the same sort of delicate curlicue furniture his mother favored.

She was in her lounge and stood on something because she was a foot taller than normal. He couldn't see what it was because her wedding gown was belled over it, flaring a meter in each direction. A filmy veil was draped over her dark hair and all of it was covered in more seed pearls than there were in the ocean.

Fatina rose from her chair and came to kiss his hand, tsking as her older daughter charged at him, arms raised in a demand to be lifted and hugged.

Kasim concentrated on setting down his one sister and lifting the eight-year-old so she could squeeze his neck with her skinny little arms and press her lips to his cheek.

"You're growing too fast," he told her. "You'll be wearing one of these soon and then who will draw me pictures? You look very beautiful, Hasna."

He set down his sister and pretended he was taking in the extravagance of the gown when he was far more focused on the flash of movement behind the flare of her skirt.

The veil rippled slightly and Angelique rose, her attention remaining stubbornly fixed on her creation.

His heart skyrocketed as he took in the graceful drape of her pink dress and the way she'd covered her head in an ivory scarf so she looked like she was a part of his world—

She turned her head to meet his gaze.

The mercury shooting to the top of his head stalled and plummeted.

Trella.

He didn't know how he knew. The resemblance was remarkable and he couldn't say that her eyes were set closer or farther apart, or that her face seemed wider or thinner. He just knew this wasn't Angelique, even though her greenish-hazel eyes stared at him.

Given the antagonism he sensed coming off her in waves, the straight pins poking out of her mouth were unabashedly symbolic.

He knew how she felt. He was ready to spit nails himself. Where the hell was her sister?

"Angelique has done an amazing job, hasn't she?" Hasna said. He could hear the lilt of trickery in her voice, hoping to fool him.

"I understood this to be a collaboration between the twins. Hello, Trella. It's nice to meet you. Is your sister here?" He looked around the lounge, returning to a state of tense anticipation.

"Oh! You can't tell this is Trella!" Hasna accused. "I can't. I still think this is Angelique and she's tricking me."

Trella pinned a place on the veil that she had marked with her fingers, then removed the rest of the pins from her mouth to say lightly, "I showed you my passport."

Hasna chuckled and Trella glanced at Kasim, smile evaporating.

"She went back to our suite."

He couldn't stop staring, feeling as though he was looking at a film of Angelique. She was a faithful image of her sister, but there was a sense of being removed by time or space. She made him long to be in the presence of the real thing.

"Still recovering from her flu?" he said with false lightness. "Perhaps she should have stayed home after all."

"It was minor. She's over it." Trella's glance hit Kasim with pointed disparagement.

Did she recall that he had done her a favor, hiding her night with the Prince of Elazar? An attitude of deference wouldn't be amiss here, he told her with a hard look, but he didn't have time to teach her some manners.

He had to get her sister on the next plane back to Paris.

Angelique was normally at her most relaxed around her family, but not today. She was wound up about being here, feeling like she was smuggling drugs, that pouch of Jamal's was so heavy on her conscience.

Ramon was not helping. He was growing restless away from work and began badgering her to play tennis.

"I thought Henri said he would?" She was actually

dying to see more of the palace. As they had come in by helicopter with Sadiq's family, Angelique had been awestruck. And taken down a peg. What had made her think she had any place in Kasim's life when his home sprawled in opulent glory over more area than a dozen football fields against the stunning backdrop of the Persian Gulf?

She told herself that it was the heat of the desert sun that caused her to sweat as they were taken by golf cart along a palm-lined path overlooking a water feature. It was actually anxiety. Kasim was here. Somewhere behind those columns and tall windows, beneath the domes and flags, he was carrying on with his life, perhaps already having moved on to another lover, completely unaware she had defied him and come to Zhamair after all.

She searched across the gardens, noting small gatherings in gazebos and colorful tents, trying to see if he was among any of the groups. Guilty and eager at once for a glimpse of him.

Maybe she wouldn't see him until the wedding. She'd been trying to decide whether to contact him outright and request a meeting prior to the wedding—and probably be asked to leave—or just hope she came across him and was able to say her piece before he deported her.

Being special guests of the groom and traveling with the groom's parents, her family was given a luxurious suite of four rooms with a stunning stained glass window set high on the exterior wall of the lounge. It poured colored light onto the white tablecloth of the dining table, where fruit, cordial, sweets and flowers had been waiting on their arrival.

"Gili!" Ramon said. "Are you listening?"

"Are you? I said you and Henri should play. I have to

hem these for Hasna's sisters." She lifted the silk dresses she'd brought back from Hasna's suite.

Fatina had cried when Hasna revealed that her daughters hadn't been overlooked in the wedding preparations.

Now that Angelique had met Jamal and had an even broader understanding of the family's painful dynamic, she was thrilled to be part of including Fatina's children in the wedding. And, as much as it pained her, she had accepted payment from Fatina for them. Fatina had insisted, worried what the queen would say if she didn't. Angelique had kept it very nominal, doing what she could to keep the peace.

Ramon sighed.

"You have to come with us so we can talk to any women we meet." He spoke like he was explaining it to a child. "I don't know how Sadiq survived these restrictions," he muttered, resuming his pacing.

Ah. It wasn't work he was missing so much as his extracurricular activities.

"Ask Mama to go with you," she suggested drily.

"Siesta or I would," he shot back. "Desperate times."

She shook her head at him.

Henri emerged from his room. He had changed into light gray sweatpants and a white long-sleeved tunic. He made a small noise of disgust as he saw that was exactly what Ramon already wore. They didn't try to dress alike, but it happened constantly. Even their panama hats had been purchased on two different continents, but their tastes were so in sync, they had each brought one to Zhamair.

When they set them on their heads, they did so facing each other, moving like mirror images—because that's what they were. She and Trella were stamps, both right-handed, both wearing their hair parted on the left because that's where their crowns were.

The boys were left and right, but were still difficult to tell apart for most people. They wore their hair in the same short, spiked cut, favored the same clothes and had such even features they easily passed for the other, not that they played that game.

Well, Ramon had tried with Cinnia a couple of times, because he was a tease, but she had always caught him. Her ability to tell both sets of twins apart from the get-go was one of the reasons Angelique had been so sure Cinnia was right for Henri.

Her brothers left and she sat down to work.

A knock sounded a few minutes later.

Most of Trella's security detail were women so they'd been given much-deserved vacation time, rather than coming to work where they would have been hampered in performing their regular duties. When the family was together like this, in a secure location, they needed fewer guards anyway.

Maurice was outside this door and she paused to listen, expecting him to ask for identification.

Nothing.

Weird. Unless he already knew the person knocking?

Angelique faltered, suddenly paralyzed with nerves, then forced herself to rise and open the door.

She caught her breath.

He looked so exotic in his *bisht* and *gutra*.

She had studied menswear to design her brother's wedding cloaks, but even though she'd taken great care with them, Kasim's was obviously of royal quality and tailored by hands that were intimately familiar with the engineering of such garments. His robe fit his shoulders perfectly. It was stark black with its V opening trimmed in gold, his white *gutra* framing his face and secured with a cord of matching gold.

He had let his beard grow in, but it was trimmed to a sexy frame that accentuated his mouth and the hollows of his cheeks. The contrast of white and black and gold made his eyes look all the more like melted dark chocolate.

He stole her breath.

His expression flashed something that might have been exaltation as he looked at her, but it was quickly schooled into the stern, confrontational look he'd worn the day she had met him.

"You can't be here," he said.

She searched for the woman she'd been in her office that first day, the one who had stood up to this man, but it was far harder to find her backbone when he looked right through her and saw all her weaknesses.

Her weakness for him.

Somehow she managed to speak despite the earthquake gripping her.

"You'll feel differently when I tell you what brought me here."

Instantly alert, he stepped in, crowding her into stumbling backward. His expression was grave as he firmly closed the door behind him and left his hand flat on the carved panel. His lips barely moved as he said in an undertone, "Pregnant?"

"What? *No!*" Her heart fishtailed, then did it again as his mouth tightened.

Disappointment? *Don't be stupid, Angelique.*

He smoothed his expression into something aloof and pitiless, sweeping his gaze around the empty lounge. He tensed and swore under his breath.

"Are you alone?"

As his gaze slammed back into hers, practically knocking her onto her back, her skin tightened with anticipation and a rush of heat hit her loins.

"My m-m—" How was she supposed to speak when he looked at her like that? "Mama is asleep in her room," she blurted, pointing to the one closed door. "Trella will be back any minute." *Quit making me think you still want me.*

His nostrils flared and he swung away, moving into her lounge like he owned it, which he did. He cast a glance around to take in the litter of tablets and purses, her open mending kit and his young sisters' dresses in vivid green and yellow.

"Damn you for coming," he said, pitching his voice low, but it was still overflowing with restless emotion. "What do you think you're accomplishing?"

Angelique moved to her purse and dug for the velvet pouch, hand shaking as she offered it to him.

Kasim hadn't been able to stop thinking about how they'd ended things, the bitterness of it. He hated that the acrimony would be even deeper after this. He had lived in that sort of thorny forest all his life and knew how unpleasant it was.

That Angelique had forced his hand and was making him reject her outright, forcing her to leave his country, seemed cruel on her part—which was the last word he would use to describe her. He hadn't expected this of her and that made it doubly hard to accept and behave as he knew he must.

Yet there was only the anticipation of pain as he stood here. Duty and reputation hung like anvils and pianos over his head, but in this moment, the bleak anger that had consumed him had become radiant light in her presence.

Angelique turned, expression solemn, and stood where the stained glass poured colors over her golden skin and pale blue dress.

He drank in the picture she made. Memorizing it.

Then she offered something to him and her expression was so grave, so filled with deep compassion, it made his heart lurch. All the hairs on his body stood up as he took the pouch and poured its contents into his hands.

He recognized the workmanship if not the piece. New. Better than anything else he'd made yet. His brother had definitely found his calling in this.

The piano landed.

She knew.

"Your family knows this is why you came?" His mind raced while cold sweat lifted in his palms. He tried to imagine how he would contain this, but his mind was as empty as the shifting dunes in the desert. Old protectiveness warred with fresh, fierce aggression while betrayal washed through him.

"No," she dismissed, barely speaking above a whisper. Her eyes stayed that soft, mossy green. "They think I decided to brave the wedding. That's all."

"How did you find him?"

"He came to me. Asked me to bring that to you for Hasna."

Trella walked in, making both of them start guiltily. Kasim let his arm fall so his sleeve fell over his fist where he clutched the pendant. He slipped it into the side pocket of his robe.

Trella's gaze flicked between them, sticking upon her sister's pale face. "Shall I come back?"

"No," Kasim said on impulse, probably a self-destructive one. "You can tell your family that she's with me." He clasped Angelique's hand in an implacable grip.

"Kasim—"

"We have to talk." He had to ensure Jamal would stay dead. That's what he told himself, even though he knew at a cell-deep level that he could trust Angelique with this secret. She hadn't told her family, had she?

"Gili, your phone," Trella urged, handing it to Angelique as Kasim tugged her toward the door.

There's no point, he thought, as he decided on the fly where they were going.

CHAPTER TEN

A LIFETIME OF taking precautions and Angelique had been kidnapped anyway. Maurice had been left in the dust. Fat lot of good her panic switch would do a hundred miles into the middle of nowhere.

But they were *some*where. As the helicopter lowered into an oasis, tents fluttered under the wind they raised.

Kasim was in the copilot's seat and unhooked his headgear as they settled on the ground, glancing back to signal she could do the same. The whine of the rotors slowed and dwindled.

"No wonder you were so offended by my audacity that first day." She leaned to see more of what looked like a scene from an epic Hollywood tale of Arabia. "You are a future king, Kasim. I didn't fully appreciate that."

"I am aware," he said flatly, crouching to circle in front of her and push open the door. He leaped to the ground before holding up a hand to help her exit.

This strong hand had spirited her down a servant stairwell that had felt like a secret passageway. She had allowed it because she had expected to come out in a library or private lounge.

They had wound up in a break room of some kind where men watched TV and read the paper. One had been eating a rice dish. They had quickly stood to attention when Kasim appeared, all plainly shocked so she assumed he never went there and never with a woman whose head was uncovered!

They'd leaped to do whatever Kasim ordered in Arabic and moments later he had tugged her upstairs and out to the helicopter.

She had balked and he'd said, "Get in or I'll put you in."

What was she going to do? Set off her panic switch and an international incident? He wasn't going to hurt her. He didn't want to extort money from her family.

"Are you flying me out of Zhamair? At least let me get my passport."

A muscle had pulsed in his jaw. "We'll be in the desert."

We. For some reason that had been enough to make her climb into her seat. Minutes later, they'd been chasing their own shadow across the sand.

Now they were at their destination, a pocket of verdant green in an otherwise yellow landscape that was turning bronze with the setting sun. Palms loomed over the tents that showed not the tiniest ripple now the rotors were still. The water mirrored the scene, placid and inviting.

People moved, however, bustling out of one of the biggest tents to stand at the door, heads lowering with respect as Kasim drew her into it.

"This is…" There weren't words for the fantasy of draped silk and tasseled pillows that surrounded her. Candles had been lit and an erotic incense perfumed the air. A low table with cushions for chairs was set with what looked like gold plates and cutlery. In the distance, music from a lute began.

The bed was low and wide, draped with netting so

it was a tent within a tent, sumptuous in its bold colors and swirled patterns on silk sheets, luxurious in its multitude of pillows.

"Where will you sleep?" she asked pointedly.

He gave her the look that said, *Take care.*

"Well, you're taking a lot for granted, aren't you? You may be a future king, but I am not some harem girl you can order to your bed for the night."

Listen to her, talking so tough when she might as well be a concubine stolen by a barbarian for all the power she had here. And for all the strength she had when it came to resisting him. She was already reacting as she always did, hyperaware of his physique as he shrugged out of his *bisht* and tossed it aside.

He wore a light *thobe* beneath and peeled off his *gutra*, running a hand through his hair, letting go of his veneer the way she had often seen him do when they entered a private space. He was shedding the future king to reveal the man who captivated her.

"Have you ever *been* a harem girl?" he drawled. "If not, it should be a treat for you to try it. You can dance for me later."

She was standing near the door with her arms crossed, and did her best to dice and slice him with her stare, but found herself fighting a laugh. *The bastard.*

"Don't you dare act like this is funny. My brothers will be beside themselves."

"So will my father. What was that expression you used after your sister's antics? Ah yes. They can grin and bear it." He slouched into the only chair, one with wooden legs, sumptuously cushioned in blue velvet with matching pads on the arms.

Oh, this banter felt familiar and inviting. Poignant.

She wanted to let all the harsh edges between them soften.

She couldn't. He had hurt her and could again, so easily. She ducked her head, avoiding letting her gaze tangle with his.

"Why did you bring me here?"

"Because my father wanted you removed from the palace." He indicated she should move. She was in the way of the servants bringing food.

Forced to step deeper into the tent, she watched as dishes of fruit and bowls of something that smelled rich and spicy were set out for them. When they finished, they looked back at him for further instructions.

He sent them away with a flick of his wrist, as supremely arrogant as Angelique had ever seen him.

Tipping his head against his chair back, he watched her through eyes so narrow his lashes were a single black line.

She shifted her bare feet under the skirt of her dress. Her phone was still in her hand, showing zero bars of coverage. He hadn't let her pause for a scarf or sandals.

"I would make you my harem girl if I could. Keep you here. That's how my father started up with Fatina. This is her family."

"This is their tent?" She glanced at the bed, not sure how she felt about that.

"This is my mother's. She used it once when they were first married. She doesn't like the desert. I use it."

"Ah." Of course. She scratched beneath her hair where the back of her neck was damp from perspiration. At least the sun was setting. The heat was beginning to ease.

"After me, my mother was reluctant to have another child. I don't judge her for that. I watched Fatina go through several pregnancies and she carries like she's made for the process, but it still looks cumbersome."

Cumbersome. How enlightened he sounded. She bit her lip against interrupting with sarcasm. The way he was being so forthcoming had her staying wisely silent, curious to hear how much he would tell her.

"When Fatina became pregnant, my father married her. If it was a son, he wanted him born legitimate. An heir and a spare. Mother was incensed. She promptly got herself pregnant with Hasna. She and Jamal are only a year apart. That's why they were so close." He had his elbow propped on the arm of his chair and smoothed the side of his finger against his lips. "My father was ambivalent toward Hasna. Still is. He sees little value in females. They are expensive."

"She's so sweet," she was compelled to say. "It's his loss he doesn't appreciate her."

"It is. And I often think that for all the nightmare his having two wives has been, at least she had Fatina. Mother was quite content to shuffle her newborn onto Number Two. The messy years of wiping noses and offering affection. She enjoys Hasna's company now, but if mother had raised her, we would have had two shrews terrorizing the palace, I'm sure."

What a way to talk about his mother.

"If she was thrown over because she was afraid to go through childbirth again, can you blame her for her jealousy? Does he love Fatina? That must have been a blow to her, too."

"She didn't have to turn into what she did. After Jamal, she quietly fed Fatina birth control pills for years. My father was furious when he found out. He knew by then that Jamal would never—" Kasim's mouth flattened, face spasming with anguish.

"He told me," she said, pulled forward a few steps on the silken rug that covered the floor, then halted and curled her toes against the cool material. *Jamal wouldn't marry and produce an heir.* That's what he had been about to say. "It's terrible that your father couldn't accept him. Was his life really in danger?"

She didn't want to believe it. Who hated to such a magnitude?

"From my father's intolerance, my mother's jealousy, and latent bigotry in some of our countrymen, yes." His hand fisted on the arm of his chair. "Do you think I would have taken such extreme steps otherwise? Even I couldn't risk seeing him."

He was so impassioned and tortured, she was drawn forward another couple of steps. At the same time, she wondered if Jamal was still in danger and glanced toward the door.

"They have some French, but don't speak English. And they'll have given us our privacy by now."

Privacy? For what? She was here to talk. That's *all.* Wasn't she?

"How was he?" Kasim's voice was low and yearning, hopeful, yet worried. When she met his gaze, she saw that same search she had seen in Jamal's eyes. He longed for news of his family.

"Good. I think," she reassured, smiling with affection because she had been quite taken with his brother by the time they'd parted. "Homesick, maybe, but he seemed content. I gave him my private number and begged him to collaborate with me on something, but I realize it might be too risky. I won't tell a soul, Kasim. I swear."

He dismissed that with a flick of his hand.

"I know you won't, but it may not matter. If I give Hasna that necklace... His body wasn't found, obviously. She and Fatina have held out hope. I had to give them that much. But what now? Do you know how much it has weighed on me that I hurt them like that? My father is no dummy and neither is my mother. Do I come clean? Put his life in danger again? What the hell do I do, Angelique?"

There was so much torment in his expression, her insides twisted painfully and her eyes welled. She threw herself into his lap and slid her arms around his neck, hearing his breath rush in as his chest filled. He clamped hard arms around her and squeezed her into the space against his torso, allowing her to drape her legs over the arm of the chair, then snugging her even tighter into the hollow of his body.

The way he held her pressed more tears out of her so she sniffed and tucked her wet cheeks into his throat.

"Don't cry," he said. "It's not for you to weep over."

"I'm crying for you," she said as a little shudder racked through her.

"I am fine, Angelique. My life is not in danger. At worst my father could disown me. I'll survive."

She drew back, thinking that men were so obtuse at times. "I'm crying *for* you. Because you can't. Can you? Have you ever let go of any of this?"

His brow angled with great suffering and his mouth tightened. "No," he admitted, and pressed her head to his shoulder. "No, I never have."

Fresh agony rose in her, spilling from her eyes and releasing as soft, pained sobs.

He stroked his hands over her back and arms, throat swallowing against her forehead, tension easing as he held her and held her while she cried. She cried for him and for them. She cried because he was leaning his heart against hers and his was so heavy, so very heavy, and she wanted to brace it forever, but she knew he wouldn't let her.

He was strong and disciplined and had responsibilities to a *country*. She might have room inside her for him, but his life did not have room for her.

Which meant it was pure self-destruction to slide her hand from his neck down to where his heart beat. Setting her damp and salty lips against his throat was both a step out of the pain she'd nursed since their breakup and a willingness to go back to a deeper level of it.

"I missed you," she confessed, because if she didn't say that, she would say something else. *I love you.*

He brought his hand to the side of her head and tucked his chin to look into her eyes. "I missed you, too."

His face spasmed anew. "But I still can't make you any promises."

"I know." It was a knife, twisting in her heart, but she only said, "We're together now, though. Even if it's only for an hour, Kasim…"

He groaned and she tasted the longing in him as he covered her mouth with his.

Joy quivered through her, blocking out the future and fear of loss, brimming her with happiness at being in his arms again. Pain ceased and all was right in her world.

They kissed without hurry, breaking away to look into each other's eyes, caress a cheekbone or the shell of an ear, then returned to another kiss of homecoming. She couldn't get enough of him. There would never be enough.

He rose, keeping her in his arms, and moved to the bed where they stretched out alongside each other with a sigh of relief. Together again, at last.

He jerked back. "I don't have condoms. I don't bring women here. I'll have to ask—"

She touched the side of his face. "I'm on the pill. It's okay."

"You never told me that before." He frowned.

"PMS makes me really emotional. That's the only reason I take them."

She would have pointed out that she didn't have them *here* because she hadn't been given an opportunity to pack, but he smiled and kissed her again, which distracted her from anything but how wonderful it was to lie with him again.

When he drew her onto her side so he could unzip her dress, there was reverence in his touch. He took his time, took great care as he stripped her dress down to her waist and unhooked her bra. She tugged it away herself and tossed it aside, smiling as he gave her breasts the possessive, hungry look that tightened her skin all over her body.

Heat pooled between her legs and she had to press into his groin with her own, *had to.*

"You have missed me," he said with satisfaction, cupping a swell and lowering his head to capture her nipple.

She gloried in the sensation, unable to get close enough to him. As her dress rode up, so did his *thobe*. She scraped her legs against his hair-roughened ones and used her hand to climb the fabric higher. His thighs were hot steel, but she was seeking that other column of strength.

He abruptly pushed onto his knees and threw off his *thobe*, revealing his sculpted form, the dark tone of his skin seeming extra dark as the light faded.

"You were naked under there," she commented, a little dazed by the idea. Her gaze slid past his six-pack to the thrust of his erection, so aggressive and familiar.

She was compelled to reach out, claim and squeeze.

He was velvet over steel, smooth and damp at the tip. She wanted that turgid heat moving inside her, soothing and stoking.

"Ah!" He reacted with a clench of his abdominals and fisted his hand over hers, eyes glittering fiercely at her.

"I will have my way with my harem girl first," he told her, thrusting in her grip a few times before peeling her hand off him and leaning to press the back of her hand to the mattress above her head. Then he tugged to remove her dress and underwear. "So many wicked pleasures…"

He stroked his hand from her collarbone over her breast to her hip, arranging her to best please his eye.

"Kasim." She writhed, loins clenching and aching as he skimmed his touch past her sensitive folds. She tried to guide his touch back to where she wanted it. "Please."

He caught her hand and tucked it beneath the small of her back. Then he gathered the other and did the same as he rolled atop her, using his legs to part her own.

"Don't tease," she protested. Caged beneath him, she rubbed her inner thighs against his, lifting her moist center to invite the penetration she longed for.

He shifted down a few inches and stayed propped on his elbows, admiring the way her hands beneath her back arched her breasts to him.

"Better," he said, and cupped both, lifting them for his delectation. He licked and teased and sucked, moving back and forth between them until she hugged her knees to his ribcage, shamelessly offering herself, *begging*, "Kasim, *please.*"

He laughed and smoothly slid down even farther, licking at her very lightly, just once. She was so aroused, she had to catch back a cry.

"Don't be shy," he ordered, drawing a circle with his fingertip. "No one is listening but me. Do you like this?"

He pressed a finger inside her and tasted her again as he did.

She groaned in encouragement.

"You do," he said with satisfaction, and pressed two fingers inside her, making her moan with intense pleasure as he set about lavishing such attention she quickly shuddered with climax. Oh, she had missed him so much.

"So beautiful," he told her as he kissed his way up her belly. "You please me very much, my little harem girl."

"Your harem girl is going to tell you to go to hell if you don't quit calling her that," she panted.

He chuckled and rolled to her side, allowing her to free her arms, caressing himself with two fingers as he looked at her sprawled next to him, slumberous from climax, but aroused and filled with desire for him.

"Do you want me to do that to you, My Prince?" She rolled into him so her breath was humid against his chin. She nipped lightly. "Would you like me to please you with my mouth until you can't even speak?"

"Yes." He gathered a fistful of her hair, holding her still for his kiss, pressing over her and parting her legs with his, thrusting in and shuddering, lifting to look into her eyes as they absorbed the feeling of being joined without a barrier between them. "Later," he breathed. "Later I want you all over me. I want you to ride me and give me your nipples and I want you on your knees in front of me. I want you every way I can have you."

"I'm yours," she vowed. "All yours."

For now.

CHAPTER ELEVEN

"I'VE NEVER SKINNY-DIPPED BEFORE."

"No?" Kasim wondered how she was swimming at all. He was worn right out, barely able to sit upright on the natural rock ledge that hung just below the waterline.

He was exhausted, but knew he wouldn't sleep even if they went back to the tent. And he didn't want to miss a moment of her slick form twisting in the inky black of the water, rippling the reflection of the moon and stars. His midnight mermaid. He would remember this forever.

He wanted this night to last forever.

"Tell me something else about yourself," he coaxed.

"Like what?"

"Something about your childhood. Before." Before her sister's kidnapping he meant, when she had been carefree.

"Um…" Her voice hummed across the water like a musical note. "Oh, this is something not many people know. My father spoke French and my mother spoke Spanish, even when they spoke to each other. The boys grew up thinking that if Mama spoke to them, they had to reply to her in French and Spanish with Papa. If they spoke to each other, Henri used French and Ramon used Spanish. Then we came along and did the same thing."

"That's ridiculous."

"I know. The boys knew better by then, but they thought it was funny. We girls grew out of it once we realized it wasn't normal for other families."

Thinking of herself only as a piece of the collective wasn't normal, either. He wondered if she realized *that*.

"Now tell me something that is just about you," he commanded.

A pause, then a dreamy, but rueful, "I like birds."

"Which ones?"

"All of them. I'm weirdly fascinated and have dozens of books about them. I listen to recordings of their songs and study the patterns of their feathers. I love that they fly and always know where they're going. I'm intrigued by how they build their nests and I always imagine that when I'm old, I'll be one of those odd people squatting behind a log with binoculars, excited because I can tick off red-throated warbler in my birding book. Are you laughing at me?"

"That would make me a hypocrite. I own falcons."

The water rippled as she let her feet sink and brought her head up, swirling around to look at him. "Really?"

He had to smile at her excitement. He suspected he had just won her over for all time. For good measure, he added, "My mother has an aviary."

"Can I see it?" She skimmed closer in her excitement, then paused to tread water. "Never mind. I'd probably cry because they're caged."

He held up a hand to warn her as he noticed a servant coming toward the shoreline.

The report didn't surprise him. Nor did the apologetic way it was delivered. Fortunately he was too relaxed to order a beheading of the messenger.

He responded with a flat "Thank you," and jerked his head to indicate they should be left alone again.

"What was that?" Angelique asked, turning to watch the retreat.

"My father is not grinning and your brothers are not bearing." And he was not interested in talking about reality. They had stepped beyond time, at least until morning. He wished to enjoy it.

"Relaying my safe word didn't reassure them?" She sounded genuinely surprised. Small wonder.

"I didn't relay it."

"Kasim! Don't do that to them." She swam a little closer.

He reached out his feet, but she was too far away to catch and drag close. "Your sister knows you came with me willingly. What do they think I'm going to do with you?"

"Just tell them I'm all right," she said impatiently, looking again to where the servant had disappeared.

"My father knows where I am. He can arrange to transport them here if they need proof of life so badly."

"Or you could send a message."

"I'm just as happy to let them pressure him into having you returned to the palace."

"You're using me," she said with a lilt of outrage. "Using *them* to back your father into a corner. I thought you didn't play those games." She made a V in the water as she headed away from him, toward shore. "What would that even accomplish? He can still disinherit you, can't he? Are you going to risk that so I can stay for the wedding? For *one* day?"

She was really asking if he was fighting for a broader future with her. And she was right that he would be disinherited for *that* sort of transgression. He was playing a dangerous game as it was, thinking he could steal this night with her.

"Why can't you just enjoy what we have?" he challenged. That's what he was doing.

"I *was*. Sex and skinny-dipping is great. But apparently I'm not here for that. You want to punish your father. You're using me to embarrass him because you're angry about Jamal." As she climbed from the water, her shoulders hunched, even though the air was still velvety and warm.

"Stop accusing me of only wanting sex from you." He pulled himself up and out, pushing to his feet so water sluiced off his naked body in a trickling rush. "I brought you here because this is where I'm happiest. I wanted you to see it."

He waded along the ledge until he reached the path on the shore, then he circled through the high grass to where she stood, towel wrapped around her middle, arms hugged over it.

"Will you take me back? Please?"

"To the palace? You're going to choose a night with your family over one with me? Live your own life, Angelique! Quit hiding behind your sister."

She recoiled like he'd taken a swing at her.

"This *is* me. I don't hurt the people I love."

"Meaning I do?" Now who was delivering the sucker punch?

She dropped her gaze so he only saw her pale eyelids, not whatever emotion might be glimmering in her eyes.

"You're better at holding yourself apart from things. I even understand why you had to become that way. But I feel things, Kasim. Do you think I came to Zhamair for a midnight swim in an oasis? No. I came because my heart was torn apart by a family so broken I couldn't stand it. I came *despite* knowing I would probably wind up in your bed and be shattered at having to leave it again."

"Then *don't*," he growled, hating to hear that he was hurting her when it was the last thing he wanted to do. He thought of her sitting in his lap, crying for him, and his guts twisted.

"And what?" she challenged softly. "Become Wife Number Two? Look how well that turns out!" Her profile was shadowed with despair as she gazed over the moonlit water.

He sighed and pinched the bridge of his nose. The last time they'd had this conversation, he had fought to exclude one day from their lives. Now he saw the single day they might steal—only a night, really—slipping away.

"You want me to call your brothers with your code word, *fine*."

"Your father will still know I'm out here and resent it. Do you really want to fuel the fire? I don't want to be the reason you two went to war the day before your sister's wedding. Kasim, I *love* you."

The words struck him with such a blast of heat and light, he rocked back on his heels, speechless at how powerful the statement was.

"I know you don't feel the same," Angelique rushed to say, appalled that she had spilled her heart out at his feet like that. Crushed that he only stood there looking stunned. How could he not have expected this?

"I don't *want* to know how you feel," she added quickly. "It would make this even more impossible to deal with," she babbled on, drowning in yearning. "But that's who I am. If you think I hide behind my sister, it's because I don't know how else to protect myself from feeling so much. You get past even that and it makes me feel so defenseless."

She wanted to look at him, but was afraid what she'd see. Pity? Weariness with yet another woman falling at his feet?

"You *could* talk me into being a second wife, and we'd both lose respect for each other for it," she said, feeling as though one of his falcons had taken her chest in its talons and was squeezing relentlessly. Her voice thinned. "So I'm asking you not to wield your power over me. Be the man I love and show respect for someone weaker than you. Don't use me in your fight with your father. Take me back and make peace with him for your sister's sake."

He let out a breath like she'd kicked it out of him.

"Don't be selfish like my parents," he summed up, voice as dry and gritty as a wind off a sandstorm. "You should give yourself more credit, Angelique. You're plenty brutal when you need to be."

He took her back to the palace and let her go without so much as a reluctant "goodbye." She didn't suppose she would ever forgive him for that, even though it was exactly what she had asked for. She had hoped for some kind of miracle though. Foolishly hoped.

Henri met her off the helicopter and escorted her wordlessly back to their suite where she half expected Ramon to be waiting up. He wasn't. They were all asleep.

"Is Trella okay?" she asked as Henri firmly closed the door behind them.

"*Bien*. She's your champion. You know that." He unstoppered a bottle, smelled the contents, and set it away with disgust. "Cordial. How do they survive without a decent brandy? Do you want to tell me what you were thinking, disappearing like that?"

She lifted a hand and huffed out a breath of despair. "Do you want to tell me what went wrong between you and Cinnia?"

He jerked his head back. *"Non."*

She tilted her head. He knew how she felt then. Sometimes things were far too painful to share.

He sighed and held out his arm. *"Je m'excuse, Gili.* Come here. I hate fighting with you. It just makes me feel like a bully."

She laughed faintly. "Because I don't fight back?"

"You just did. Most punishingly." He hugged her. "But it tells me how hurt you are when you hit below the belt like that."

"I'm sorry about you and Cinnia," she murmured as she hugged him back. "It's so hard to find people we can trust. Even harder to keep them," she added in a voice that thinned to a whisper.

He squeezed her and set her away. "You should get some sleep. We may be packing to leave first thing."

They didn't. Kasim pulled strings and Angelique was allowed to stay for the wedding. At least, she assumed Kasim had arranged it, until she and Trella caught up to the bride to help her dress.

Hasna had been crying, as most brides were wont to do, and was running late while her makeup was fixed. Her suite was being cleared, everyone leaving to take their seats. Angelique offered Fatina a smile as the woman hurried past her, but Fatina didn't even acknowledge her. She was ashen beneath her olive complexion. She looked both wispy and frail, yet had an incandescent glow behind the wetness in her eyes.

Angelique's blood chilled with premonition, but she was pulled back to Hasna's reflection as she spoke.

"I told Mama to tell Papa I want you both at the wedding. I realize there are politics, but…" She touched the pendant at her throat and Angelique wondered if there were other reasons for the smudged mascara and puffy eyes, the haunted shadows behind Hasna's somewhat shell-shocked expression.

Oh, Kasim. Angelique wished, illogically, that she could have been with them when he'd given Jamal's gift to his sister, to hold his hand and bolster him as he had made his explanation.

"That's fine," Hasna said with a flustered dismissal of the makeup artist, sounding very much the princess as she said, "*Go.* I just want to be married and live with my husband. Help me dress."

The woman left and Angelique and Trella helped Hasna into her gown. She was a vision, with a distinct line of maturity setting her shoulders and running like a line up her spine. Some might see it as her wedding causing this coming-of-age moment, but Angelique knew it was the necklace she kept touching. The memories of time lost with a cherished brother.

It was another tear in the fabric of Kasim's family and Angelique silently ached for all of them.

"I don't think I've ever been prouder," Trella said, linking her hand with Angelique's. "Oh, look at you, crying over how beautiful she is! Our tender little Gili. We used to call her Puddles. She hated it."

Her sister was being Trella, giving Angelique an excuse for the tears that were filling her eyes because yes, she was proud of their work, but she was bombarded by so much emotion in this moment. She hurt for Hasna and Fatina, Kasim and Jamal. At the same time, she saw the dress as a symbol of what had brought Kasim into her life. It was exactly what she would never wear when walking toward him. In fact, today especially, she couldn't go near him. In future, it would be far too painful to approach him, not that she expected to bump into him anywhere.

The wedding reception was the last time she would ever see him and she wanted to weep openly with her loss, until she collapsed in a heap.

Trella squeezed her hand in comfort, as though she felt the echo of agony that clenched Angelique's heart.

Hasna's bouquet dropped an inch and her come-and-go smile faded into misery.

"You have both worked so hard to make this day absolutely perfect and—" Her gaze briefly met Angelique's, but she quickly shielded her thoughts with a sweep of her lashes. "I can't believe I have to ask you for another favor. Sadiq will kill me if he knows, but my mother wants a picture of the three of us. She said it's about the dress, but I know it's because she's excited to have the first photos of you both together in public."

Hasna looked embarrassed and angry, but resigned.

Angelique glanced at Trella, worried the photo request was too high a price. If Trella wanted to refuse, she would back her up, even if it meant they were both expelled from the wedding, the palace and Zhamair.

Even though it would mean not catching a last glimpse of the man she loved.

Trella smiled even as her fingers tightened on Angelique's.

"Of course," Trella said. "I knew photos would wind up in the press and I'm only sorry it might overshadow your special day. But if you're not bothered by that, then I'm not. You, Gili?"

Angelique shook her head and tried to bolster Hasna by saying, "Anything for you, because you make Sadiq so very happy. You know how much we want that for him."

Hasna's smile returned, shakily, then beaming with anticipation. She blinked. "Yes. He's lucky to have such good friends. Me, too." She touched her pendant and nodded. "I'm ready."

When it came to levels of power, there were elected officials, religious leaders, authoritarian dictators and right at the very top of that heap: Mother of the Bride. When she also happened to be a queen, she accomplished great feats with a single sentence.

"You cannot expect Hasna to give up the prestige of hosting such rare guests for a woman who may or may not join this family." Her tone implied that she would veto Kasim's prospective bride completely if she impacted the illustriousness of Hasna's day.

His mother didn't know the reason Hasna had become so insistent on having *all* of The Sauveterre Twins at her wedding. Kasim had gone to see his sister last night, when he'd returned from the desert. She had known the moment she saw the pendant that Jamal was alive. "You would have shown this to me before, with all the rest."

As the truth had come out, she had railed at him, and cried bitterly, but she understood that it had been Jamal's choice, and the people truly at fault were their parents. He hoped she had managed a few hours of sleep after that. He hadn't, too aware that Angelique was close, but essentially gone from his life.

Then, just before the ceremony, he had held out his arm to escort Fatina to her place behind the king and queen. She had been trembling, her face a stiff mask, as she'd said, "I saw what you gave to the princess."

Her eyes had held a maelstrom of emotion, topmost resentment and betrayal, but underscored by a glittering return of hope.

He would owe her some explanations, too, he supposed. At least he was able to brood unnoticed as the attention through the reception was drawn in a completely different direction.

Watching the wedding guests behave like the twins were creatures in a zoo made Kasim sick. They had all been briefly introduced at the receiving line, Angelique removing her hand from his like the contact had burned. Her eyes had remained downcast and his heart had been a tortured knot from the moment he saw her coming to the moment she'd disappeared into the crowd.

Her brothers now bookended their sisters, Henri on Trella's right, Ramon on Angelique's left, all posed in a row like movie stars to allow photographs, the men wearing dark green, the women a lighter shade, so all their eyes flashed like emeralds. Their smiles were aloof and unbothered.

They *were* a sight, so very good-looking, tall and flawless and so startlingly the *same*. An old woman touched Ramon like she wasn't sure he was real. He said something that made her cover a titter and blush. Angelique sent her brother a reproving look and pinched his arm.

Kasim's lungs felt tight as he memorized the vision of her. His heart had echoed her voice through him with every pound since she'd said, *I love you.*

Respect someone weaker. Did she not know how weak she made him?

He fantasized about having a second wife. The wife he really wanted. He loved her, too.

And claiming her would make him just like his father.

He ran a hand down his face, ensuring none of this struggle was evident as he gritted his teeth and tried to get through the hours of this everlasting wedding.

A servant touched his arm. "You must come," he said. "The king."

What now? Kasim stalked after the man, taking a relieved breath as they went through a door and the worst of the noise was closed out behind them. "Where is he?"

"The doctor is with him in the Consort's Chamber."

"Doctor?" Kasim's heart lurched. He strode past the man up the stairs to more quickly reach Fatina's suite.

Her rooms were at the far end of the wing from the royal apartments, but it didn't surprise him that his father was there. It did shock him to find his mother coming toward the same door from the other direction, expression tense. Fatina's maid was trailing behind her, obviously having fetched her with the same urgency.

This was serious.

Kasim's mind raced. Should Hasna be called away from her guests? Was it that bad? He pushed into the lounge and found his father being loaded onto a stretcher, an oxygen mask over his gray face. He wasn't conscious.

"What happened? What have you done?" The queen was quick to accuse Fatina.

Not her. Me, Kasim thought.

Fatina was crying, tail end of her scarf bunched up to her mouth, shoulders shaking with sorrow.

"Why was he even here when he should be downstairs with his guests? *You*—"

"Mother," Kasim said through his teeth. He looked to the doctor.

The royal physician wore a very grave look. "We will do what we can. Perhaps the queen should accompany us in the helicopter."

For potentially his father's last moments. Kasim's insides clenched.

As they all looked to Kasim for direction, he thought about the guests downstairs. The woman he'd used to needle his father—not to score points, but because he loved her.

The end result was the same, however. He had given his father a heart attack.

Kasim felt not just the weight of decisions that would have to be made in the next five minutes, but the weight of a nation landsliding to rest with infinite weight upon his shoulders. Even if his father recovered, Kasim was the man in power until he did.

And he didn't deserve it.

He had thought his father's censure had hung heavily around his neck. His own self-contempt was worse.

"Mother," he prompted. The word stuck in his throat. "I will follow with Hasna as soon as we can." And Fatina. He wished he could give her the honor of flying with the man she loved. She was rocking in her chair, face buried in her scarf as she tried to stifle her sobs.

Turning to a servant, he ordered them to have Hasna and Sadiq wait for him in one of the anterooms downstairs. He would tell them first, then make the announcement.

And he would say an unspoken, but final goodbye to Angelique.

I don't want to be the reason you two went to war the day before your sister's wedding.

Nevertheless, she was. She would never see this differently and neither would he.

Do you need me? I will stay if you want me to.

Angelique had rather foolishly sent the text as the wedding fell apart and Kasim disappeared, presumably to have a police escort to the hospital where his father was struggling to hang on to his life.

He didn't respond. Not that day, not before she left Zhamair, not as his nation went into mourning at the news of their king's demise, and not after his father was laid to rest and Kasim was crowned king.

She followed all of it, doing exactly what she had told him once she would never do. She stalked him online and even read what was said about the two of them, reliving their various moments together, not caring about the inaccuracies and wild theories and outright lies.

As one week turned into two, then three and more, it became obvious that he didn't need her. He took his rightful place on the throne and seemed fully in control of all he surveyed. Infinitely resilient and autonomous.

Now she felt vulgar for having sent the text in the first place. All she had wanted was to reach out to him in that moment when he must have been so anguished, but who was she to think she had anything a *king* could need?

It hadn't struck her until afterward that her presence at the wedding might have been the catalyst for his father's heart attack. Kasim had been so remote as he'd made his announcement that the king had been taken to hospital, so very stately and contained, yet she had sensed his agony.

Now she wondered—did he blame himself? *Her?*

She wished she hadn't been so quick to climb on her high horse at the oasis. She should have stayed there with him. No, that was selfish. It might have made things worse with his father. Of course, how could the outcome have been any worse than death? Still, she had been so preachy when really, she had been doing what he had accused her of. She had hidden behind her family because she loved Kasim so deeply, it scared her.

And leaving without having spent a full night at the oasis didn't mean she hurt any less now.

She hurt for both of them, so much so she went online yet again and walked straight into a statement from a source "close to the king." A marriage was being arranged and an announcement would be forthcoming.

She couldn't tell if it was an older statement made by his father or something Kasim might have said recently.

Either way, it rattled her all over again and drove her away from looking at any kind of screen for days.

She had to get on with her life.

But she couldn't make herself go back to Paris. She had come to Spain from the wedding, to lick her wounds, allowing her mother to mollycoddle her now that Trella was so much better and spending the bulk of her time in Paris.

Trella had finally confided a few details about her night with the Prince of Elazar to Angelique and was dealing with the fallout from it—big fallout—but she was fiercely determined to handle things alone and not lean on her siblings again, particularly her twin. It was both admirable and worrying, but Angelique had to let Trella muddle through and just impress on her sister that she was here if she was needed.

Even though she felt as useful as a milquetoast.

Thank God they had Sus Brazos, the family compound. "Her arms," it meant, referring to the safety of their mother's arms. They had taken to calling it that when Trella had retreated here.

Trella might have come to see the family stronghold as a prison, but Angelique needed it rather desperately. The gated compound overlooked the Mediterranean, ever inspiring with its expansive view. The buildings were a gleaming white, the main villa obscenely luxurious and up-to-date even though it had been built when her parents first married. The staff were all such long-time employees they were a type of extended family.

It made her feel safe and cosseted in every way, which allowed Angelique to relax as she ate quiet meals with her mother, walked the gardens, sunbathed and sketched, turned in early and tried to heal her broken heart.

The days were very predictable here, which was part of its charm. And it was also why she was so stunned when she was interrupted while watching seabirds diving into a churning pool out on the water. She had a guest at the gate, she was told.

"The King of Zhamair."

CHAPTER TWELVE

ANGELIQUE WORE A summer dress in pale pink with tiny ivory polka dots. It had a high neck, but bared her golden shoulders and accented her slender waist and long legs, falling in layers of tall slits and sharp points. Her hair was in a high ponytail and she pressed her lips together over what he suspected was a fresh coat of lipstick. She seemed breathless as he was shown into their lounge.

"Welcome," she said, pressing her palms together. "My mother isn't here, I'm afraid. She had a luncheon with friends. She'll be sorry she missed you. Shall I order coffee? Your Highness?"

Kasim felt like it was their first meeting all over again. She was treating him like a stranger and was too beautiful for words, emptying his mind of all but base masculine thoughts. His perfectly tailored suit felt too tight.

Still, he found himself letting out his breath, relieved to finally see her, but exasperated by the fact he'd had to chase her down in Spain when he'd expected to find her in Paris.

"Excellency," he corrected absently. "And no to coffee."

Her mouth twitched, probably thinking he sounded

pretentious. She had never been particularly impressed by his station, which was part of her charm for him.

She sent a jerky nod to dismiss the maid and said, "Let me guess. You'd prefer to stand?"

"I would. Why is that funny?" he demanded as he heard the tiny noise she tried to stifle. "I've been sitting for hours, traveling to Paris then here."

"Paris?" The news arrested her.

"To take Fatina to see Jamal." It had been a bittersweet joy to embrace his brother again. As he'd met his brother's partner, and left Fatina to reunite with her son, Kasim had felt as though his last barrier to being with Angelique had been removed.

But now, as he entered the inner sanctum of her world, and recalled how she'd been treated like a museum exhibit at his sister's wedding, he wondered if he was taking too much for granted. The wife of a king was not exactly a low-key profile. Why would she want to take on such a position? He was struggling with the elevation in circumstance himself and it was only one notch.

"He does live in Paris, then? I wasn't sure," she said.

"Hmm? Oh. Jamal. No, he doesn't. It was complicated." A cloak of weariness fell over him. He wanted to throw off his *gutra* and shave his beard and be the man of lesser responsibilities he'd been when they'd first met.

But he was king now. And was expected to marry.

"It has been a very complicated, demanding few weeks."

"Of course. I'm so sorry about your father. I should have said—"

"Your mother's card was among the rest," he cut in. "My mother appreciated the gesture."

"She must be devastated. And poor Hasna, to lose her father on her wedding day. How is she?"

"Grieving. We all are. They curtailed their honeymoon." But he was glad his sister had such a stalwart support in her husband. It was one less weight on his own shoulders.

Angelique nodded, mouth pouted as though she wanted to say something, but knew there was nothing to say. As she looked at him, her eyes brimmed.

"Don't." He flinched, took a step toward her, then veered away, running a hand down his face in frustration. "I'm so tired of tears, Angelique."

She swallowed, trying to choke back the emotions swamping her. But she couldn't take it in! He was *here*, and so blindingly handsome. His eyes were dark and unreadable, but riveting. His mouth was stern, tension pulling at that sexy mouth of his.

He wore his beard, precision trimmed to frame his face, and also his *gutra*.

He had come to her world, but still had one foot in his.

Her heart panged because she felt firmly shut out of that side of his life. Shut out of all of it, really.

She drew a breath, but didn't know what to say.

He looked her over in the way he did sometimes, like he was taking in her hair or clothes or the set of her shoulders or the angle of her foot, but really, he was seeing what those things revealed. Like he was reading her. Seeing *her*.

It made her feel so transparent it was painful. She struggled to hold on to her composure. "This is just really…confusing. I'm not sure why you're here."

"After ignoring your text, you mean?"

She shrugged a shoulder, cheeks stinging with embarrassment all over again. "It wasn't appropriate of me to send it. I realized afterward that our going to the oasis may have contributed…" Her voice dried up. She didn't want to think she was to blame for his father's death.

"Maybe it did." His shoulders lifted and fell. "I certainly believed I'd killed him when I was being crowned."

"I'm so sorry," she whispered, hating herself for being his weakness, the thing that he'd gone after to the detriment of his father and his relationship with him.

"He had a heart condition. His heart had been failing for years." His mouth curled with irony. "But I didn't respond to your text because I blamed myself for his death. I blamed *us*."

Her worst nightmare. Her heart plummeted. There went the small dream she had formed at his arriving here, the one she hadn't really let form.

"I even blamed you for bringing that damned necklace from Jamal. I was not the man you asked me to be," he said with self-disgust.

And this was his punishment. The ultimate sacrifice, losing his father. He wasn't trying to dump that on her shoulders. She saw he carried it alone, but she felt awful all the same. Wanted to help him.

"What I didn't know, until he was dead and I was king, was that Fatina had fought with him that night herself. I was so busy in those first days after he passed away, it was two whole weeks before I could sit down and talk with her privately about her future. She fell apart, completely racked with guilt."

"They fought about Jamal?"

"She told him she wanted a divorce. I won't break her confidence by repeating all she told me, but… I do believe he loved her in whatever way he was able. Losing her, realizing he had lost her love by failing Jamal, was more than he could bear."

"But he had a heart condition," she hurried to repeat. "Please tell me you didn't make her live with that guilt."

He cast her a look that demanded some credit.

"I told her she was a generous wife and a good mother. I was unsurprised she would fight for the happiness of all my brothers and sisters, particularly Jamal. I told her she shouldn't blame herself and that I wanted to arrange for her to see Jamal as soon as possible."

"You're a good man, Kasim."

He made a dismissive noise. "I would have preferred to bring Jamal home, but I don't think that would be safe yet. I'm afraid to resurrect him. But I was able to reach him through the jeweler and we met him in Paris. He says hello and that he is still interested in working together if you are."

"That's why you're here? To deliver his message?"

"No." He gave her a look that suggested she was dense, then paced across to the windows that looked out on the sun-drenched sea. "I am here because I am under a great deal of pressure to go through on the promise I made to my dead father, to marry the woman he chose. But if I succumb to an arranged marriage, I know I would take you on the side and turn into him."

He slashed his hand through the air.

"I will not repeat history. I will not have you end up hating me as Fatina did my father. Not when I need your love so badly. I *will* need that love in the years to come, to keep me human. Ruling a country is not easy."

"Kasim…" This was heaven and hell wrapped up in one moment. She dropped her head so she wasn't looking at him. She was so tempted. "If you loved me—"

"Angelique. Look at me."

She lifted her head. The fierce determination in his features made her heart skip while the tenderness in his eyes stole her breath.

"What have I learned from my family? You love who you love. If you fight it, if you try to force it in another direction, there will be nothing but pain. You asked me once to give you up for the sake of my country. I'm coming *after* you for the sake of my country. Without you, the one I love, I will be as frustrated as my father. I'll become bitter and my heart will shrivel into a pitiless husk. Save my people from that. Save me from turning into that."

She let out a small laugh. "You're overstating, aren't you?"

"No. I watched it happen to him. He was much kinder in my youth, but his being trapped with my mother while wanting Fatina twisted him."

Her ridiculously tender heart pitied his father for the position he'd been in. Still, "Would your country have accepted her if he had married Fatina?" She'd seen Fatina's family. They were modest people of the desert. "I don't want to be a source of unrest in your country. I have a reputation, true or not. People will think you should have found someone more upstanding."

"In choosing my wife, I will be the authoritarian that my father was," he said with a point at the floor. "I will not compromise. I could engage myself to the woman he chose and tomcat through Europe for the next four years until I marry her, but I don't want that sort of freedom. I don't *want* other women. I don't want *her*. I want *you*. I will have you. My uncle and my advisors and anyone else who disapproves can…" He showed his teeth. "Grin and bear it."

She couldn't take it in, especially now she'd seen the scope of his life. If she had thought being a media darling was onerous, she couldn't imagine flouting his country's conservatives and becoming his wife.

"I'm not someone who thumbs their nose at the establishment. They'll tear me apart."

"They'll try." His mouth tightened. "But you'll win them over. God knows you'll be well protected until you do. I swear to keep you safe, Angelique."

"But you're overestimating what I'm capable of."

"Like hell," he said softly. "You think you're only brave if you pretend to be your sister. You are bravest when you're defending her because you *love* your sister. That love of yours is such a well of strength. I've seen it and I want it beside me, supporting me. I know that *my* love for *you* will make me a better man. Provided I can indulge it," he added with a look that was both sensual and tender.

Oh, he was such a seducer. Her heart fluttered like a caught bird and her eyes stung with moved tears. She cupped her hot cheeks.

"How could this be a surprise to you?" he chided, coming toward her and increasing her excited turmoil.

He took her wrists and drew them down so they stood face-to-face. She had no way to hide how overcome she was.

"I didn't think you loved me," she confessed in a daze. "I thought maybe if we had had more time you might have come to care…"

"I *care*," he admonished. "I always cared. And I am not someone who needs a lot of time to know my own mind." He shifted his grip and caressed the back of her knuckles with his thumbs. "But we will have to take things slow. Announcing an engagement this soon after my father's death— You're not pregnant, are you?" he asked with a sharpening of his expression.

"What? No! How could I be?"

"We didn't use anything at the oasis."

She huffed out a disbelieving laugh. "I'm on the pill, remember?"

His mouth twisted. "Shame. It would have given us a reason for shortening our timeline, but it's probably for the best if we do things in the right order." He sighed. "I want to make so many changes in my country, relax restrictions and change attitudes, but it has to be done carefully or there will be chaos. Is that the reassurance you need, Angelique? You will have time to put all these pieces together in your pretty head."

He was teasing her, reminding her of their first night together when he had tried to railroad her into extending their affair. She wanted to duck into him, maybe have a little cry because this was so much to take in. She was trying to smile, but her lips were trembling.

"I didn't bring a ring. I asked Jamal to make one for you."

She had to choke out a little laugh and pull one hand free to swipe at a tear that leaked down her cheek. "You don't have to *bribe* me."

"No? Well, I brought this anyway, hoping it would be an inducement." He released her other hand and reached inside his suit jacket, bringing out a velvet box she recognized.

Her heart did a little bump and roll as he flipped the lid to show her the emerald necklace he'd tried to give her in Paris.

"I should have explained that day that it was not a pay-off. Jamal made this years ago, before he left Zhamair. I told him that one day my queen would wear it."

"Queen!" Her knees wilted and Kasim quickly hooked his arm around her, catching her into him. Which didn't help at all because finally being back in his arms was such a relief she melted against him completely.

"What did you think?" He leaned to drop the necklace on the side table and scooped her under her knees, moving to sit on the sofa with her in his lap.

"I just wanted you to love me. Yes, I had fantasies we might marry, but because I want to be your *wife*. I want to see you every day and share my life with you."

"Finally she says yes."

She curled her arm around his neck and laugh-cried against his throat at his presumption. *So* like him.

But she loved him. So much.

Tipping back her head, she set her trembling hand against his bearded cheek, gazed into his beloved eyes and said, "I would be honored to be your wife."

"And my queen."

"Harem girl, if that's what you need me to be," she said, barely able to see him, her eyes were so full. She swiped at her silly leak of tears. "Good thing I had no time for makeup. I'm trying not to do this, you know. You said you were tired of tears, but I'm just so *moved*."

"The sad tears are killing me. The angry ones. I trust these are happy ones?"

"They are. Oh, Kasim." She lifted to press her mouth to his, unable to hold back her expansive feelings.

His arms tightened to gather her closer and he kissed her with deep passion and infinite tenderness. Love imbued the moment, sending a rush of joy and heat through her. Desire. That delicious, sharp desire that only he ignited in her awoke to make her burn.

He was reacting just as instantaneously. She felt his

hardness against her thigh and he slid to press her beneath him on the sofa.

As his mouth slid down her throat, he lifted his head and frowned at her bare neck. "No panic button."

"I wasn't going to put one on for *you*."

"Even though I intend to steal you from your family?"

"That part will be hard for me," she admitted. "It's good I'll have time to do that in stages. But there are times when I'm impatient, you know." She loved the feel of his stubble against her palm and absolutely had to trace his bottom lip with her thumb. "I don't want to go to a hotel," she whispered.

"No?" He was reading the hunger in her and answering with a growing heat in his own gaze. He shifted so he was between her legs, pressing his hardest flesh against her softest.

"It will take too long to drive there and have it scouted. I want to sneak you into my bedroom so you can ravish me there. *Now*."

He pulled away, drawing her up as he went. "See how good you are at encouraging me to compromise? Lead the way, my beautiful future wife."

EPILOGUE

Two months later...

ANGELIQUE WAS ALWAYS happiest when her whole family was together, but she felt a little guilty for being *so* happy today. It was her engagement party, however, so she was entitled to be elated.

And it wasn't a huge party, which made her even happier. Just those closest to them gathered at Sus Brazos for a weekend to celebrate what amounted to a secret engagement since they weren't officially announcing it for another few months.

She was making other people happy with this small party, too. Sadiq and Hasna were here and Jamal had just arrived with his partner. Kasim was sequestered with the four of them while his brother and sister took a few minutes to reunite in person after being in touch again since the wedding.

It gave Angelique a few minutes to study her sister, who was arguing heatedly with Ramon on the far side of the pool. Of the four of them, those two were the only combination to descend into yelling matches. They weren't there yet, but it was only a matter of time before one of them completely lost their temper and pushed the other into the water to cool off, evening clothes notwithstanding.

The way Henri was glaring at them, it might very well be both of them taking a swim—by his hand.

"What's going on?" Kasim asked, coming up behind her and wrapping his arms around her waist.

"They have Mama's hot Spanish blood." She leaned back into him. "Henri and I have our father's French temperament, you lucky duck. Our silence speaks volumes. Their volume does."

"What are they fighting about?"

"Unclear and probably not important," she said with a fatalistic sigh. She suspected Trella had picked this fight to let off steam. Her sister was troubled. Angelique had been feeling it, but couldn't do a thing about it. Trella was being that delightfully frustrating shade of her true self: stubborn and ferociously independent.

She had even come up with a plan to transition Angelique from the day-to-day operations at Maison des Jumeaux, while allowing her to keep her foot in the door, submitting designs and indulging her artistry around her duties as queen—oh, she would never fully grasp that!

Trella was determined for Angelique to move on with her life without feeling held back. It made Angelique wistful, even though she was also grateful. She loved Kasim so very much and wanted to be with him without guilt.

"How is Hasna?" She turned in his arms to ask the question.

"Good. They'll be out in a moment, but I couldn't wait to show you... Come here."

He pulled her a little farther along the veranda to a corner where the light was soft and the view was nothing but starry night and glittering sea. The fragrance off the early summer blooms came up from the garden below and the warm air caressed her bare shoulders and calves.

She had a feeling she knew what he wanted to show her, but was still overcome as her future husband caressed her arms before he went down on one knee.

"Angelique, my love."

"Oh! You don't have to do that." She instantly choked up and lost sight of him behind a film of emotive tears.

"Arrêtez," she heard Henri growl at her siblings, receiving instant silence. She suspected they were being watched.

She was never comfortable as the center of attention, but she looked into the face of the man she loved and knew he would keep her safe no matter what.

"Will you marry me?" He showed her the ring that Jamal had made, the one she had been holding her breath to see. Now, in this deeply moving moment, she couldn't make herself look away from the love in Kasim's eyes.

"You know I will. I love you with everything in me. Please." She waved for him to rise. He was a king after all.

He did, suddenly tall and close. He slid the ring on her shaking hand and handed her his handkerchief so she could clear her vision enough to fall in love with the hint of a feathered design cut into the band. Claws like talons held a stunning round diamond. It was simple and elegant, pretty, but imbued with the fierceness of her husband while conveying that he did know her very well and longed to please her.

"I *love* it."

"I love you." He cupped her chin and kissed her tenderly. "This time next year we will marry in Zhamair. It's far too long to wait, but this is a step in the right direction."

A small burst of applause made them both glance in that direction and she blushed to discover not just her mother and siblings, but Jamal and his partner, Hasna and Sadiq, all beaming at them.

They would marry in a ceremony that would be big and overwhelming, and her life would be equally huge and daunting, but she would have these cherished people to help her through it.

And this man. She looked up at Kasim, her other half. Not her reflection, but her complement. Curling her arms around his neck, she went up on tiptoes to kiss him.

* * * * *

If you enjoyed this story,
look out for more scandalous tales of
THE SAUVETERRE SIBLINGS
coming soon!

In the meantime, why not explore these other
great reads from Dani Collins?
THE SECRET BENEATH THE VEIL
BOUGHT BY HER ITALIAN BOSS
THE CONSEQUENCE HE MUST CLAIM
THE MARRIAGE HE MUST KEEP
VOWS OF REVENGE
Available now!

MILLS & BOON®

MODERN™

POWER, PASSION AND IRRESISTIBLE TEMPTATION

Just can't wait?
Buy our books online before they hit the shops!
www.millsandboon.co.uk

Also available as eBooks.

MILLS & BOON®

EXCLUSIVE EXTRACT

Stefano Moretti wants only revenge from his wife, Anna. When she reappears after leaving him, with no memory of their marriage, he realizes that this is his chance…for a red-hot private seduction, followed by a public humiliation! Until Stefano realizes there's something he wants more than vengeance—Anna, back in his bed for good!

Read on for a sneak preview of
ONCE A MORETTI WIFE

Stefano pressed his thumb to her chin and gently stroked it. 'When your memories come back you will know the truth. I will help you find them.'

Her heart thudding, her skin alive with the sensation of his touch, Anna swallowed the moisture that had filled her mouth.

When had she given in to the chemistry that had always been there between them, always pulling her to him? She'd fought against it right from the beginning, having no intention of joining the throng of women Stefano enjoyed such a legendary sex life with. To be fair, she didn't have any evidence of what he actually got up to under the bedsheets; indeed it was something she'd been resolute in *not* thinking about, but the steady flow of glamorous, sexy women in and out of his life had been pretty damning.

When had she gone from liking and hugely admiring

him but with an absolute determination to never get into bed with him, to marrying him overnight? She'd heard of whirlwind marriages before but from employee to wife in twenty-four hours? Her head hurt just trying to wrap itself around it.

Had Stefano looked at her with the same glimmer in his green eyes then as he was now? Had he pressed his lips to hers or had she been the one…?

'How will you help me remember us?' she asked in a whisper.

His thumb moved to caress her cheek and his voice dropped to a murmur. 'I will help you find again the pleasure you had in my bed. I will teach you to become a woman again.'

Mortification suffused her, every part of her anatomy turning red.

I will teach you to be a woman again?

His meaning was clear. He knew she was a virgin.

Anna's virginity was not something she'd ever discussed with anyone. Why would she? Twenty-three-year-old virgins were rarer than the lesser-spotted unicorn. For Stefano to know that…

Dear God, it was *true*.

All the denial she'd been storing up fell away.

She really had married him.

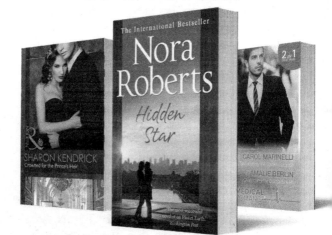

MILLS & BOON®

Congratulations
Carol Marinelli
on your 100th Mills & Boon book!

Read on for an exclusive extract

How did she walk away? Lydia wondered.

How did she go over and kiss that sulky mouth and say goodbye when really she wanted to climb back into bed?

But rather than reveal her thoughts she flicked that internal default switch which had been permanently set to 'polite'.

'Thank you so much for last night.'

'I haven't finished being your tour guide yet.'

He stretched out his arm and held out his hand but Lydia didn't go over. She did not want to let in hope, so she just stood there as Raul spoke.

'It would be remiss of me to let you go home without seeing Venice as it should be seen.'

'Venice?'

'I'm heading there today. Why don't you come with me? Fly home tomorrow instead.'

There was another night between now and then, and Lydia knew that even while he offered her an extension he made it clear there was a cut-off.

Time added on for good behaviour.

And Raul's version of 'good behaviour' was that there would

be no tears or drama as she walked away. Lydia knew that. If she were to accept his offer then she had to remember that.

'I'd like that.' The calm of her voice belied the trembling she felt inside. 'It sounds wonderful.'

'Only if you're sure?' Raul added.

'Of course.'

But how could she be sure of anything now she had set foot in Raul's world?

He made her dizzy.

Disorientated.

Not just her head, but every cell in her body seemed to be spinning as he hauled himself from the bed and unlike Lydia, with her sheet-covered dash to the bathroom, his body was hers to view.

And that blasted default switch was stuck, because Lydia did the right thing and averted her eyes.

Yet he didn't walk past. Instead Raul walked right over to her and stood in front of her.

She could feel the heat—not just from his naked body but her own—and it felt as if her dress might disintegrate.

He put his fingers on her chin, tilted her head so that she met his eyes, and it killed that he did not kiss her, nor drag her back to his bed. Instead he checked again. 'Are you sure?'

'Of course,' Lydia said, and tried to make light of it. 'I never say no to a free trip.'

It was a joke but it put her in an unflattering light. She was about to correct herself, to say that it hadn't come out as she had meant, but then she saw his slight smile and it spelt approval.

A gold-digger he could handle, Lydia realised.

Her emerging feelings for him—perhaps not.

At every turn her world changed, and she fought for a semblance of control. Fought to convince not just Raul but herself that she could handle this.